HILDA BROOKMAN STANIER

◆

PLANTAGENET PRINCESS

Complete and Unabridged

LINFORD
Leicester

First published in Great Britain in 1981 by
Robert Hale Limited
London

First Linford Edition
published 2006
by arrangement with
Robert Hale Limited
London

British Library CIP Data

Stanier, Hilda Brookman
    Plantagenet princess.—Large print ed.—
    Linford romance library
    1. Elizabeth, Queen, consort of Henry VII,
    King of England, *1465 – 1503* —Fiction
    2. Love stories 3. Large type books
    I. Title
    823.9'14 [F]

ISBN 1–84617–413–9

Published by
F. A. Thorpe (Publishing)
Anstey, Leicestershire

Set by Words & Graphics Ltd.
Anstey, Leicestershire
Printed and bound in Great Britain by
T. J. International Ltd., Padstow, Cornwall

This book is printed on acid-free paper

Prologue

PLANTAGENET PRINCESS

Elizabeth of York is a controversial figure. Did she or did she not love her Uncle Richard? What was the relationship between herself and Margaret Beaufort, her mother-in-law? How much affection did Henry VII have for the niece of the man whose throne he had usurped by right of conquest? This book attempts to answer these questions and gain an insight into the life of Elizabeth of York.

Edward the Fourth had ruled England for nine years.

Henry of Lancaster, the deposed King, weak of mind and pious of nature, dominated by his Queen, the Frenchwoman Margaret of Anjou, was now imprisoned in the Tower while Margaret and her little son Edward had fled back to the unwilling protection of Louis, King of France.

It was the battle of Towton, where for two days the beck ran red with the blood of York and Lancaster, which finally established Edward upon the throne, and his chief supporter was his cousin Richard Neville, Earl of Warwick, whom the people of England had named 'The Kingmaker'. This man held a great deal of power but as time went on the King decided to take more control of the kingdom into his own hands and this decision did not go down well with Warwick's ambitions. He saw his position as Edward's chief adviser threatened and as a result he became more and more a thorn in the King's side, questioning all aspects of Edward's rule.

Gradually, the friendship between the two men became so strained that Warwick realised he had gone too far, and, in 1470, seeing that Edward's patience was at an end, he fled secretly from England with his wife and two daughters, Isabel and Anne.

Accompanying him was George, Duke of Clarence, who had married Isabel Neville and who coveted the throne.

Louis of France was a devious monarch, unfriendly to Edward, and he saw in Richard Neville the means whereby he could overthrow the Yorkist King and at the same time be rid of his unwelcome guest, Margaret of Anjou. So he offered the Earl of Warwick gold and troops if he would sign an alliance with his old enemy Margaret, return to England, depose Edward and replace Henry of Lancaster upon the throne. This was agreed to and shortly afterwards Warwick set sail, leaving Margaret and her son to follow when he had established a foothold on England's shores.

Edward advised of the Earl's landing at Plymouth, hurried his Queen Elizabeth Woodville and her three small daughters into the Tower and rode to confront Warwick.

Part I

The Child

Elizabeth of York stood in the richly appointed chamber, watching the scene before her.

Through the arrow-slit windows of the palace within the Tower the sun cast its dying rays, picking out the figures of Queen Elizabeth Woodville, the two younger children, Cicely and Mary, clutching nervously at the Queen's skirts, and the maternal grandmother, Jacqueta of Bedford, together with the ladies in attendance upon the Queen.

In that darkening room, the atmosphere was heavy with uncertainty and dismay, and the anxious child longed desperately for some measure of reassurance.

For as long as she could remember her days had been passed in luxury amid the busy hum of her father's court behind the stout walls of Greenwich,

Eltham, Windsor, and Westminster where she had been born. In these great palaces Edward the Fourth's glittering court had moved, a pageant of colour and elegance unknown in the time of Henry of Lancaster. Everywhere had moved familiar figures, uncles and aunts, knights and ladies, pages and serving-men, heralds who came and went, jesters darting about in parti-coloured costumes, all dominated by the figure of her father and the radiance of her beautiful mother presiding over the subservient courtiers.

But now a great change had taken place.

The Queen standing in the chamber where none had thought to bring torch or candle stared through the gloom at the Mayor of the City of London.

'How plebeian he looks,' thought Elizabeth Woodville, 'waiting there in his scarlet hose, his cap askew upon his head, his mayoral chain dangling about his skinny neck.' He was one of Edward's merchant friends, a grocer, elevated to his high position by her appreciative husband and she remembered that to Edward the common man meant a great deal.

Realisation stabbed her and she saw that this man was the only one who could help her in this terrible situation.

'Master Lee, what is to become of us?'

The Mayor's eyes rested upon the productive figure of the King's consort.

'She is over eight months with child. Pray God she does not miscarry at this time,' he thought, then his mind returned to the Queen's question. What indeed was to become of them?

Outside the walls of the fortress the waves of sound beat like a distant sea, ebbing and flowing as the howling mob raided alehouses and taverns, pillaging everything in its path. Thank God he had been able to close the gates of the City and the damage so far had been confined without its walls, but the way things were going how long could he hold out?

With the Queen stood her fluttering ladies, three frightened children and the only composed face among them was that of Jacqueta, Duchess of Bedford. Much had been whispered of this mother of the Queen — devil worship, sorcery, spell-making — but now she appeared to Richard Lee as the most rational being present as she spoke resolutely,

'Master Lee, what is that noise? Surely the Londoners have gone mad.'

The Mayor shook his head.

'Nay, Your Grace, it is not the people of London who menace us. The Earl of Warwick is responsible for this. After the King had left the capital the Earl, evading him, rode in and sent orders that all Lancastrians held in Southwark gaol were to be freed. But with them escaped all the criminals and it is this rabble who now strive to take possession of the City.'

The ears of the listening child caught the name of the Earl of Warwick.

'Was he not her father's friend,' thought Elizabeth. 'Many a time he had tossed her on his knee and brought her sweetmeats. How could he be responsible for all this violence?'

Elizabeth Woodville passed a hand over her feverish brow, her mind turning to her husband.

The last time she had seen him was when he bade her farewell here and had set out to confront Warwick. Since then news had come through only of Richard Neville's unopposed advance towards London and his proclamation that he came to take possession of the City and replace the Lancastrian King upon the throne.

It was the Mayor who spoke now in anxious tones.

'You must flee into sanctuary, Your Grace. Only then can you avoid being captured. If you will relinquish the Tower into my control, I will do my best to defend it until I hear from the King.'

Elizabeth shook her head.

'I fear to pass through the streets,' she cried.

'No need,' he answered swiftly, 'your barge stands at the watergate. Take only what is needed and make for the wharf of Westminster. Once there the abbey will receive you into sanctuary.'

The Queen, the Duchess and the agitated ladies scurried about the rooms, throwing back the lids of heavy chests to cast neatly packed robes, capes, veils and headdresses into colourful heaps, while Elizabeth of York watched, clasping the hands of her sisters. Eventually, burdened with their possessions, they made their way down the stone steps awash with water to where the royal barge waited, and when they had embarked the oarsmen moved off.

All along the shore, smoke interspersed with scarlet flames soared into the night sky and the leaping gesticulating figures were silhouetted like demons dancing in the fire of the nether regions, while the crackle of burning buildings came faintly to their ears.

Luckily, the mob was too busy with its own affairs to give heed to the river, and finally the barge docked at Westminster. A short journey and they reached the abbey, where they were greeted by the anxious Abbot, who, with every mark of respect, led them to their new apartments. Once there the Queen's control broke, and the casket of jewels she carried fell to the floor while their owner gave way to her distress in emotional tears.

Her eldest daughter watched with wide eyes. Was this the proud mother whom she knew so well, this distraught woman sobbing before her? Often in the past she had seen her maternal parent sitting in regal splendour while her husband's kin and the members of her own family paid homage to her. Even in their private apartments she had known always to give due deference to the lady. It was to her father that the six-year-old girl had turned for the love and understanding she needed. And where was he now?

Tears stung her eyes but she blinked them away, turning to put her arms round her small sisters in affectionate reassurance.

In the days that followed, the little girls knew small abatement of their unhappiness. They wandered about the rooms which seemed so small and dark after the space of their former homes, while their mother sat listlessly pulling at the leaves of some beautifully illuminated book from the Abbot's library and lamenting her unkind fate.

The ladies round the Queen did what they could for the bewildered children, telling them stories of King Arthur and his knights, or playing a constricted game of hoodman blind to exercise the young limbs. But they themselves were short-tempered and the two younger girls, recovering from their fears, became quarrelsome, so that always Elizabeth had to keep the peace between them.

The days went by and the news

which filtered through was of the worst.

The Earl of Warwick was now in control of the City while Richard Lee had been forced to surrender the Tower, and one day the sound of a great cavalcade passing by penetrated the walls of the sanctuary. Hurrying to the window, the incarcerated Queen and her family watched it pass. The men marched proudly in their scarlet coats, holding aloft the banners bearing the cognizance of the Bear and Ragged Staff, and riding in full armour, his charger covered in crimson velvet, came a figure whose banner the child Elizabeth recognised.

Involuntarily she cried aloud, 'It is Uncle Richard,' for so she had always called him. A smart slap was delivered upon her cheek as her mother's voice spoke sharply.

'That is your father's enemy and no friend to our house. Remember, child, Richard Neville deserves the death of a traitor and will no doubt suffer the same when your father returns.'

Holding her reddened cheek the chastened child crept away, sobbing under her breath, towards the Abbot's personal chapel. Only in the tranquillity of its setting could she forget the present and re-create in her childish mind that former life she had once enjoyed.

The holy vessels resting upon the purple velvet altar, the tall candles flickering in the dim light and, above, the great crucifix with its lonely figure of shame and glory, all gave her a feeling of comfort. It was there that Abbot Myling found her, a small figure with clasped hands, staring before her. She looked up at him, her face still wet with tears, and he placed a kindly hand upon her shoulder. Encouraged by his sympathy she spoke timidly.

'Good Abbot, will my father ever return?'

He answered her reassuringly although doubt stirred in his breast.

'Yes, my little lady. Surely one day you will be reunited with him. Trust in

God and hope on.'

The kindly words soothed her heart and she left the chapel to rejoin her family.

Time passed on leaden feet, but eventually news came that Edward had fled to Burgundy and taken refuge at the court of his sister Margaret's husband. Learning this the Queen spoke distractedly to her mother.

'Surely Charles of Burgundy will give aid to his brother-in-law. They say that my husband continually petitions for an army to aid him in the regaining of his kingdom.'

She rose to her feet as she spoke, walking restlessly about the small apartment, and the Duchess answered her sharply.

'Do not be so agitated, my daughter, or the babe will suffer. Your husband was never one to sit and repine. He will always be at Burgundy's ear to grant him the help desired.'

Disregarding her mother's advice the Queen went on, 'Let us pray that

Margaret of Anjou does not make contact with Warwick before my husband sets foot again upon these shores. I hear that Richard Neville has married his daughter Anne to Margaret's son Edward and now parades Henry through the streets of London in kingly robes. He hopes that one day he will be the father of a Queen of England if Edward of Lancaster becomes again heir to the throne.

The Duchess answered her tartly. 'The Earl has many other troubles to contend with, my child. His elder daughter Isabel is married to the Duke of Clarence now filled with fury as he sees the crown return to Henry. He did not think that he would sink to be a dependant of Warwick's. Surely to him Richard Neville belies the name of Kingmaker.'

She laughed shortly and the Queen answered her forcefully.

'George was always unstable. Richard of Gloucester, although I do not like him, is of a different metal. He is but a boy but he scorns to become a traitor.'

The Queen swayed suddenly then, speaking urgently.

'I feel pains, my mother, the babe is on its way.'

Immediately all was action. The three children were hurriedly led into another room and there, much to their astonishment, they remained, the little ones clinging to Elizabeth who but a child herself strove to comfort them, although uncertainty held her in its grip.

Soon, however, came glad news. By the goodwill of his grace of Warwick, who was a humane man, comforts had arrived to sustain the labouring Queen, while Abbot Myling visited the children, endeavouring to distract their attention from the strange sounds issuing from the bedchamber. At last they ceased and the door opened to admit one of their mother's ladies while the cry of a new-born infant fell upon their ears.

'Elizabeth, Cicely, Mary, give thanks.

Your mother is delivered of a healthy son. Surely your gracious father will be a happy man when he learns the news.'

Elizabeth bounced to her feet. 'We have a brother,' she cried proudly. 'Will our father come now to see the new babe?'

The lady's face clouded.

'I know not when that will be. But at least he has an heir, which will encourage and sustain him in his adversity.'

Shortly afterwards there came to the children a welcome break after the tedium of many weeks.

Poor indeed it was compared with the baptism of the little girls but Elizabeth proudly held the chrism and if the godparents were but two, the Duchess of Bedford and Abbot Myling, the sex of the child allowed its mother to stand in regal dignity during the simple ceremony in the Abbey. The son she needed to raise her even higher in her husband's regard was a healthy reality and the Queen was conscious of renewed hope. She would not now despair! She would set herself to the task of preparing for her husband's return and she heard with delight the Abbot's impressive voice intoning the name 'Edward.'

Only too well did she know that from across the sea, perhaps even now setting foot on England's shore, came Margaret with her son, and he, too, bore the name of Edward of England. But Elizabeth Woodville, whatever her faults, was a courageous woman and she braved the anger of the Earl of Warwick to name her son.

Following this the little family settled itself to endure confinement, hopeful that some better news would soon arrive. Slowly but in increasing volume, different gifts were arriving for them as the Queen's brave gesture found favour in the eyes of the Londoners. A certain butcher sent meat to vary their diet, a kindly craftsman made toys for the children, and musical instruments were received on which they could learn to play simple melodies. And always the Queen and her ladies attempted to tutor the children in their early lessons.

It was after Christmas that the first hopeful news was received. From Burgundy, Charles had made his decision and Edward knew he was to get the assistance he needed.

In March he set sail for England, strengthened by Burgundy's troops and accompanied by Richard, Duke of Gloucester, Anthony Woodville, his old friend Lord Hastings and many who had fled into exile with him.

Now joy reigned supreme in the Abbot's chambers. The Queen walked about, her eyes bright, her speech lively. The younger children, catching her mood, hopped and skipped through the rooms while the ladies chattered excitedly like magpies. Quietly Elizabeth of York crept up to her grandmother and put a timid hand on the old woman's sleeve.

'Is my father coming home at last?' she asked, voicing the thought that always exercised her young mind.

Jacqueta smiled down upon the young face raised so confidently to hers.

'Surely now there is great hope, my little one,' she said.

Still they waited while the news came in of Edward's arrival back in England. Of his reaching York. Of Warwick's departure from London to confront the King. Finally the tidings that George, Duke of Clarence, with his men had ridden to meet Edward and, face to face, had intimated that he regretted his past actions and wished to become once again a scion of the House of York.

Gladly he was welcomed back by both Edward and Richard of Gloucester while Warwick, sheltering behind the walls of Coventry, raged at the news.

The way to London was now open and at the tidings of Edward's approach, the City Council overruled George Neville, Archbishop of Canterbury, who held it for his brother Warwick, and took control of the capital. At the same time a message came from Edward himself, words of loving greeting to the little family in the Abbey, who found themselves caught up in a wave of expectation and delight.

Shortly afterwards they left the Abbot's lodging, riding back through garlanded streets to Westminster Palace while the people cheered and waved, giving them an ecstatic welcome. Never had they felt much enthusiasm for Henry's return and their delight was a sincere expression of their feelings.

Once again the Queen and her children found themselves installed in their former luxurious apartments and it was as if they had never left them. But poor Henry returned to his humble quarters in the Tower.

★ ★ ★

Queen Elizabeth stood in a lofty chamber in Westminster Palace, its walls covered with tapestries of velvet and brocade, the motifs, worked on linen, scattered over their surfaces in many glowing colours.

She was aware that her greatest moment was at hand, the moment when her husband would see his infant son and she would reach the pinnacle of her ambition.

When she faced him at her home in Grafton Regis after her Lancastrian husband's death in battle, her cold nature had kept the besotted Edward's ardour in check until she attained not only the return of her lands but the wedding-ring. The great prize of a crown had been well worth the simulacrum of surrender once the vows had been made.

She remembered her first husband, so loving, so kindly, to whom she had given two sons. She had needed to make no overtures foreign to her nature there, but with the sensual man now returning to his capital she must appear a different woman, suiting her behaviour to his mood and prepared in every way to satisfy the will of the King.

Outside could be heard the acclaim

of the people as they saluted their beloved monarch, and Elizabeth of York listened with delight. She waited now with Cicely and Mary, proud of her new white silk robe embroidered with gold thread and the butterfly headdress resting on her golden hair, while near at hand stood the ornate cradle where her baby brother lay attended by nurses to heed his every murmur.

At last the King arrived, that great vibrant personality, bursting into the room to stand surveying the scene with joyful gaze. Then quickly he moved forward to take the Queen in his arms.

'Elizabeth, wife.' His mouth came down greedily on hers, bruising her lips, then as three little figures came rushing towards him, lust gave way to tenderest affection and he enclosed his three little daughters in welcoming arms.

Eventually he strode towards the cradle and stood silently for a moment looking down at the sleeping infant, and his wife saw the tears gather in his eyes as pride and fulfilment pervaded his breast.

'How well you have done, my peerless Queen' he said softly — 'he is healthy?'

She answered him proudly,

'A lusty child, true son of his father.'

With a shout which penetrated to those waiting in the outer chamber the King flung his arms wide.

'Welcome to all. Now we must celebrate.'

Quickly he gave his orders and soon the members of the royal family found themselves *en route* for Baynards' Castle, where the Duchess of York waited to welcome her son. She stood elegantly to greet him, welcoming also that erring son who had so happily returned to the fold, and his wife Isabel Neville.

The scene was jubilant as the members of the House of York were reunited in the great hall of Cicely Neville's palace, the King moving among the colourful figures in his ebullient way as he accepted the acclaim which was his due.

His eldest daughter watched him with loving gaze as she spoke to one who stood beside her. 'I do not know who the lady is who stands with my Uncle George. My grandmother makes much of her.'

Richard of Gloucester answered her quietly. 'It is your Uncle George's wife, sweetheart. He has been long estranged from us, but you will soon get to know your Aunt Isabel.' And he added under his breath, 'Would you could have welcomed another aunt here also.'

He thought of Anne Neville whom he loved and who was now the wife of Edward of Lancaster.

Elizabeth scarcely noticed his last words,

'My father is so occupied he scarcely notices me,' she complained forlornly.

Richard of Gloucester smiled as he lifted her gently in his arms.

'He is overwhelmed with so much joy, but we will soon put matters right,' and moved forward.

His voice rang out above the commotion around them, calling the King's name, and the latter turned instantly, his face alight with affection.

'Dickon,' he said and made his way towards his eighteen-year-old brother.

'Your eldest daughter is discontented that you do not give her the notice she is entitled to expect.'

With an understanding laugh the King held out his arms and she was transferred into them. Tenderly he lifted her to his shoulder, walking about the hall for all to see, and the child, overjoyed, felt all was well in her small world.

The Queen also was prepared, knowing that on that same night Edward would receive from her the welcome he so ardently desired.

During all these celebrations the King did not forget that the Earl of Warwick still lurked in Coventry and that Margaret and her son, together with Anne Neville, would shortly be landing from France, hoping to join the Kingmaker.

So it was that Elizabeth of York once again waved goodbye to her father. The news had reached him that Warwick had left Coventry and was approaching London, but Margaret had not yet reached England when the two men who had once been so close confronted each other in their last battle.

It was outside the little town of Barnet that the encounter raged for three hours of bitter conflict. Cannons boomed, trumpets brayed, men and horses moved blindly in the swirling mist which covered the countryside on that early Easter Sunday morning.

At first it seemed that Warwick's forces would win the day. His troops under the Earl of Oxford had inflicted heavy losses on the Yorkists, who fled to Barnet pursued by the Lancastrians, who began looting the little town. The Earl managed to turn his men to rejoin the main battle scene, but as they approached, they met with more

Lancastrians under Montague.

In the poor light Montague mistook Oxford's banner of a star with streams for Edward's banner of the Sun in Splendour and his men loosed a hail of arrows into their returning comrades in arms. A cry of 'treason' went up and fearing betrayal, Oxford with his men retreated in disorder.

Now Edward, with the main Yorkist force, smashed into Warwick's wing, and the latter, seeing his own line crumbling and learning that Oxford had fled and Montague was slain, left the field, attempting to reach his horses waiting in Wrotham Wood.

Pursued by the Yorkists he was beaten to the ground and dispatched by an unknown hand before Edward could intervene to save his life. The victorious King now rode triumphantly back to his capital and, riding beside him, were his brothers, Clarence and Gloucester, the latter slightly wounded in the encounter.

But there was still one more enemy

to challenge his right to the throne. Margaret of Anjou had come ashore at Weymouth but, hearing of the defeat at Barnet, set out hoping to cross the Severn and reach Wales. Edward, receiving news of her landing, reassembled fresh troops and set out in pursuit.

On the outskirts of Tewkesbury, Margaret, encouraging her weary men, turned to face the enemy, her heart full of fears for her young son Edward experiencing his first taste of battle in the field. Despite their strong position the Lancastrians were too worn out to prevail and their line broke, Edward fleeing the field overcome with fear.

George of Clarence, that one-time partisan of Warwick's House, went in pursuit and pulled him from his horse. Covered with the mud of the field the boy staggered to his feet defiantly, then terror overwhelmed him. Like the fifteen-year-old boy he was, inexperienced and alone, he cried out to his former comrade in arms,

'Have pity — do not kill me.'

With a cruel laugh Clarence raised his great axe. It flashed in the sunlight and the joy and hope of Margaret's heart fell, his blood soaking the ground — and cried no more.

Edward returned then again to his capital, knowing he was now undisputed King of England, but among the many who fled across the seas was Jasper Tudor and his nephew Henry, self-styled Earl of Richmond, who had espoused Margaret's cause.

That same Margaret, but the living shell of a woman, was now carried back in the victorious King's train to join her husband in the Tower, while Anne Neville, now widowed, was given into the care of her brother-in-law, the Duke of Clarence.

Some weeks after these stirring events three young children accompanied by two of the Queen's ladies set off one morning to visit their Uncle George of Clarence and his wife.

It was a brilliant August day as the

small party made its way towards St Andrew's Hill to the west of St Paul's, the citizens respectfully making way as they waved to the rosy faces peeping out at them from the curtained litters.

Elizabeth and her sisters found it all new and exciting, and they looked with curious eyes at the comings and goings of their father's subjects.

The people jostled one another good-humouredly, the men in grey smocks, the women in dresses and cloaks, the hoods of which were lined with rabbit fur. The brown-habited monks shuffled along, carrying the sacred books of their calling, while clerks ran between the chambers of lawyers with briefs, writs and commissions. Also apprentices stood by their master's stalls, shouting in raucous voices as they drew attention to the beauty of their wares, the shimmering silk, soft velvet and gleaming satin, now being imported from Venice for the attention of the wealthy merchants' wives.

There were also laces, ribbons, bodkins, scissors, pins and purses which took the eye of the thrifty housewife while farther along the Chepe the sun caught the glint of daggers, spurs and locks, piled high on stands with leather straps, bits, bridles, and other trappings. Displayed too were metal basins, ewers, platters and all kinds of household stores.

The children found that once their progress had to give way to a procession of church dignitaries. They watched as bishops and canons walked solemnly in purple velvet chasubles with stoles of silk around their shoulders, the bishops' mitres embroidered with gold, the holy banners and crucifixes swaying above them carried by the humbler members of the clergy.

There was also a funeral to be viewed, its attendants bearing the white staves of their office, which they used to tap urgently on the ground for priority passage.

So the little group went on its way

and found themselves on arrival at their uncle's home welcomed with every mark of endearment. Elizabeth saw that her Uncle George resembled her father greatly, lacking only the King's height. The same winning charm was there to influence all whom its owner wished to attract and now he bestowed it to the full on his enchanted nieces.

The Duchess was sitting on a cushioned settle, her corn-coloured hair confined in a silk net, and as Elizabeth came to her, she put a frail hand upon the child's arm.

'I am happy to meet my nieces,' she said, but her voice was faint and there was little colour in her face.

'Have you no children of your own, Aunt Isabel,' Elizabeth asked innocently.

Isabel smiled sadly.

'Not as yet, my dear. But I hope soon to bring one to a happy conclusion.'

A shriek of laughter from Cicely and Mary drew their sister's attention, to see her uncle wrestling with the delighted little girls, and then there were comfits to be eaten, small dogs to be petted, and coloured birds in golden cages to be fed from vessels held by attendant pages.

At last the time grew near to leave and suddenly Cicely was missing. The half-open door showed whence she had gone and, quicker than her mother's ladies, Elizabeth slipped into the corridor and saw a little figure hurrying towards where the passage ended in a stout oaken door. As she reached it, the mischievous child put her hand on the latch, pushing it open and when Elizabeth joined her the two children stared into a small room where a lady rose to meet them. Her dress was simple, the small face with its startled blue eyes pale beneath the pointed hennin, then Cicely pulled the door shut, treading upon Elizabeth's toes as she retreated.

Scolding the truant child vehemently Elizabeth retraced her steps to meet the following ladies and all returned to where their uncle and aunt waited. There the elder girl, anxious to draw attention away from her sister's misdemeanour, spoke up,

'Who was the lady we saw just now? She looked so sad and lonely.'

Her uncle's face darkened and he spoke sharply. 'That is your Aunt Anne Neville who resides here, widow to the Anjou boy. By her marriage to Margaret's son she is a traitor to our house and you must have no dealings with her.'

Elizabeth wondered how one could appear so unhappy living in her brother-in-law's establishment and Mary spoke up suddenly, 'What is a traitor? So also was the Earl of Warwick.'

One of the ladies answered her forcefully. 'And so he was. A traitor is one who owes allegiance to the King and then turns his coat . . . ' her voice faded away and a deathly silence fell. Elizabeth was filled with surprise. The lady who had spoken was white to the lips while her Aunt Isabel began to weep quietly. But it was her Uncle George's face that finally claimed her gaze.

Fury mingled with shame showed upon his countenance and he spoke through stiffened lips, 'Take them away.'

Silently the puzzled children were led out and for many days Elizabeth pondered on the strange nature of their sudden dismissal. Only in later years did she understand the reason for Clarence's anger and feel pity for the position of poor Anne Neville held in durance in that household.

With the battles of Barnet and Tewkesbury behind him and the Lancastrian cause foundered, as he thought, beyond repair, Edward now set himself the task of bringing peace and prosperity to his war-torn kingdom.

He punished few, rewarded many, and gave great help to the merchants of his country, assisting them in their trade with the Continent and encouraging them to build lavishly, with glass in their windows, musicians' galleries in their halls and silver on their tables. He borrowed heavily from them but repaid the money in concessions by way of customs duties, spent freely in their shops, considered always their interests in his foreign policies and consulted them in all aspects of their trade.

So by his wise rule and the attraction of his personality he began to amass wealth both for himself and his country.

Much of this he used to refurbish his great palaces, bringing to Westminster, Greenwich, Eltham and Sheen greater luxury than ever before with gilded ceilings, priceless tapestries, and partition hangings, splendid in silver gilt thread and coloured silks, which kept out the troublesome draughts.

In 1473 he turned his attention to the rebuilding of St George's Chapel at Windsor, instructing the Bishop of Salisbury, one of the Queen's brothers, to choose bricklayers, masons, carpenters to start work on the West of the old chapel. Soon the roof of the choir rose to its full height and was roofed in while the aisles were finished so that the shields of the Knights of the Garter hung above the exquisitely carved screens, each in its allotted place.

At this time a man called William Caxton, living in Bruges and patronised by the Duchess of Burgundy, Elizabeth's aunt, was encouraged to bring his strange printing press to England and in 1476 he set it up at the sign of the Red Pale in the yard of Westminster Abbey, where it created great interest.

⋆　⋆　⋆

A hundred and twenty miles north of London stood Nottingham Castle, one of the chief seats of the King's Government. In its great hall one evening the dancing light of many candles illuminated the scene like miniature suns while on high the torches flared in iron brackets, the tongues of flame leaping and twisting toward the deep arch of the roof.

The serving-men moved about busily, replenishing the rich dishes of which at least fifty were always available to tempt King Edward and his family as they sat on a small dais before the laden board. Also well catered for were the appetites of his squires, chaplains and grooms of the chamber with their ladies, who had their seats in the main part of the hall below the great salt made of silver gilt and ornamented with mother of pearl.

The King had his Queen on his right hand, and on his left his eldest daughter. She could see down the long table where the animated faces of those close to the King sat, by virtue of their blood, rank and marriage.

Anthony Woodville, Lord Scales, now created Lord Rivers was seated opposite her, his head dutifully inclined to what his neighbour was saying, that small, stern-featured woman, Margaret

Beaufort, Countess of Richmond. Elizabeth wondered if he liked her, with her tight-lipped mouth and disapproving look.

What part this woman would play in her future life the child was mercifully unaware, deciding in her childish mind that it was only her uncle's chivalrous nature that made him listen to what the diminutive lady was saying. She expelled a little sigh as she picked up the newly favoured fork and a voice spoke beside her:

'What is this, my daughter. Surely you are not sad on such a happy evening, sweeting.'

She looked up at the familiar face above her, 'Oh, my Lord Father,' she said swiftly, 'I only study my Uncle Anthony and think how handsome he is.'

Edward surveyed the vivid little face at his elbow, so earnest beneath the delicate headdress.

'More than your own father?' he laughed teasingly.

The child clasped her hands round the velvet sleeve beside her, squeezing it affectionately,

'Oh, no,' she said, and her eyes were doting — 'You are my King as well as my father. No one could take your place in my heart. I did but feel satisfaction at his person.'

A great arm was thrown round her shoulders and a hand covered her eyes.

'I will not have my sweetest lady prefer another when I am here,' he reproved and raising his voice he shouted across the table,

'Anthony Woodville, I would take issue with you. I find you are stealing away my most precious treasure. What have you to say?'

Startled, his brother-in-law stared back, momentarily disconcerted, then understanding dawned and he rose gracefully in his place, bowing smoothly.

'Forgive me, my King. I think I rate but poorly in the heart of a certain small maid.'

A tinkling laugh from the other side of the King sounded as Elizabeth Woodville spoke,

'Would my daughter dare to take the place which is mine in my husband's affections?'

The arm round the child slid away and Edward turned his head to survey his wife. He knew that she had knowledge of the women who entered his bed ever more frequently and that it caused her little distress. There had grown up an understanding between them that as long as her position as Queen was not threatened he could have any female he desired. She had proved a cold woman and now his first passion for her had abated he turned to the lascivious appetites of many mistresses.

But she was a fertile woman, and that was what was desired in a Queen. Another son Richard had been born two years after his brother Edward, and although Mary the third daughter had suddenly died, once more a babe was on the way.

His eyes strayed over the oval face, the wide expanse of brow shaved of all hair, the beauty of flaring nostrils and full-lipped mouth, the glory of blue eyes between gold tipped lashes. Surely this Queen of his was still immeasurably lovely and he felt desire rise in him.

'You wrong yourself, as well as your husband,' he said softly, 'Wait, my lady, my enchantress, lest I chastise that elegant body.'

She laughed turning back to her trencher, and he smiled sardonically to himself, while the eyes of those around the board watched surreptitiously.

The young girl, unaware of the passing exchange between her parents, wondered why the face further down the table looked so unpleasant. What had been said to make her Uncle George scowl in such a threatening manner, and while she wondered the Duke of Clarence spoke in an undertone to his wife.

'That parcel of Woodvilles, they think

to rule the Court, and beside the King sits the Queen bee of them all.'

Isabel Neville fingered her knife nervously. She loved her husband but she was always uneasy when affairs of the family were mentioned.

The constant trouble when her sister Anne had been put into their care after Tewkesbury. The quarrel between George and his brother Richard when she had disappeared, Gloucester hinting that he had hidden her away and George denying this, saying scornfully that he had no interest in the lady and did not know what had become of her. And all this because Anne was entitled to half of their parents' lands and her husband thought that only she, Isabel, should inherit them.

The Duchess had felt great relief when Gloucester had found Anne, married her and taken her to live in his castle of Middleham in Wensleydale. But still the tension remained and she was for ever troubled by it in her delicate state of health.

Elizabeth watching down the board, was conscious of her aunt's distress.

'How pretty she is,' she thought, 'but how delicate her looks. Surely the birth of her daughter Margaret and so soon after that of the little boy Edward has drained her of much needed strength.'

Her eyes moved on to where another uncle had his place: Richard of Gloucester sitting, as he always did these days, as if his thoughts were far away, and his niece wondered what occupied his mind.

Now the King gave the word and the company was on its feet, Elizabeth joining the mingling figures. Swift servitors collected used vessels and trenchers together with boards and trestles to bear them away so that Edward and his family could reassemble upon the rostrum while the rest of the company moved about the body of the hall.

This was the part of the evening which Elizabeth enjoyed most, when the minstrels in the gallery above began to finger their instruments, causing little tremors of excitement to run up and down her young frame and set her feet tapping, while her face became bright with excitement.

Beside her sat her father and mother on gilded chairs, the King in a long blue velvet robe furred with ermine, a collar of golden suns about his massive shoulders. The Queen in a violet gown, the cuffs of glistening samite, round her elegant neck a band of golden links clasped on her breast with a great sapphire. As the dancing began, a figure in a tunic of black velvet, the Garter clasping his knee, stood before Elizabeth, hand outstretched.

'Will you dance with me, fair sweetheart,' he enquired.

Elizabeth rose daintly, laying her small hand in that of her uncle's. He was one of the most accomplished dancers at Court and gladly she joined him on the floor. As they moved to the centre of the hall she spoke shyly:

'How does your lady wife, Uncle Richard?'

Gloucester's grave face grew almost radiant as he answered her,

'Anne does very well, also our son,' and pride was in his voice, 'But tell me how you do, my little niece? It seems long since I saw you.'

Elizabeth laughed.

'If my uncle buries himself at Middleham he will never see much of me.'

The intricate steps of the dance occupied them then, but when it finished he led her back across the floor, speaking soberly,

'I control the north, Elizabeth, in your father's name. Also my heart is there with my family, I should not be here now but for certain duties which bring me to see him. But whenever he sends I must needs obey out of my love for him.'

They reached the dais where Clarence came to lead her to a gilded stool, then turned to address his brother,

'And what of my charming sister-in-law', he enquired, 'Does she still delight my brother's days as he had hoped?'

There was a moment's silence between the two, broken only by the chatter and laughter around them and Gloucester with one foot on the dais looked up into the face above him, meeting the insolent gaze with his intent grey eyes.

He spoke quietly,

'My wife is all that I could desire. But why do you ask? You have never in the past shown any concern for her well-being.'

Elizabeth's mind was troubled. She knew there had been intense antagonism between her uncles over the Lady Anne and her inheritance but she thought all had been resolved since her marriage with the Duke of Gloucester.

Now a thunderous atmosphere was engendered between the two men as Clarence jeered,

'Are you still hopeful of receiving more. You gave out that you were not greedy for her lands.'

The answer was thrown back through Richard's clenched teeth.

'Do you think it is just and fair to my wife that she should be disinherited of her lands while you claim all for Isabel?'

It was another voice which broke in then, cool and decisive, as Edward rose to his feet.

'Enough, the two of you. Do not spoil this happy occasion with your contention. This is a subject for the council chamber and should not disturb our frolic. Be silent, both of you.'

The two parted then, Richard swinging on his heel to be lost in the milling crowd, George to throw himself moodily on a bench far down the hall. It was her father's arm around her which recalled Elizabeth from her uneasy reflections.

'Do not be distressed, my daughter,' he said. 'Those two are like fire and water of late. Never do they agree over this vexed question. And yet my sympathies are with Richard. He has suffered much from George's arrogance,' he added thoughtfully.

The Queen broke in on his words, her tone scornful.

'You should give but little heed to George's words, he is not to be trusted. He carries certain bitter thoughts which sting him into resentment. As for the other,' and she flirted her hand disdainfully, 'he should cause you little concern. His interest is only in his northern lands.'

Edward's rejoinder was swift.

'Except when he considers my well-being and his wife's happiness. Richard has lately travelled from Middleham to beseech a kindness of me. He has begged me to release the Countess of Warwick into his custody. Since the death of her husband she has remained in Beaulieu Abbey from whence I have not allowed her to leave. He intends now, with my consent, to convey her to Middleham to give pleasure to his wife and more happiness to the Countess herself. Is not that a kindly gesture? I have no knowledge of George making such a request.'

The King paused, then went on gloomily, 'It seems as if of late some maggot burrows its way into his brain, causing him discontentment.'

He broke off sharply. 'But no more of our recalcitrant family. Here come the *jongleurs*.'

Elizabeth from her stool watched but with scant interest. She had seen the jesters and jugglers many times before and while they twisted and turned her anxious thoughts were far away.

Why was there always this friction between the members of her father's family? It was not only between George and Richard but between her mother's family the Woodvilles and the old nobility. It caused much enmity and dissimulation about the Court and even her father seemed powerless to control it. Therefore many occasions were darkened which should have been happy ones.

But not for long did the eight-year-old girl ponder on this problem. There was too much of interest in the life around her to wonder unduly about the older people's intransigence, and when the Court returned to London she took part joyously in the events that occurred.

Occasions when the troupes of travelling mountebanks visited the castles with their plays, many of which, lined with salacious dialogue, passed without understanding above Elizabeth's head. Hunting parties which rode out down the Route de Roi towards the great forests in the west of the capital, she riding with her father, mother and members of their two families together with horsemen to hunt the boar, the deer and the fox.

Evenings were spent in backgammon, chess, and draughts with her growing brothers and sisters and most exciting of all, days when she went with her father and Uncle Woodville to examine books from the press of Caxton. So with part of the day given over to tuition in those duties which every princess must know, life was very full for Elizabeth at this time and she lived it to the full, happily giving little thought to the miserable past and the unknown future.

About this time George Duke of Clarence, embittered by the growing power of the Queen's family and conscious that his name was impaired by his past partnership with the late Earl of Warwick, was fast turning his resentment towards his brother Richard. He heard constant reports of Gloucester's happy life at Middleham and the trust that Edward reposed in him so, true to his unstable nature, he began to intrigue against his King and brother.

Edward was well aware of the weaknesses in George's nature and he kept a wary eye on his movements. To placate him in 1474 the King bestowed a great grant of estates upon Clarence, following it up with one of equal generosity to Gloucester. He did not desire any friction at this time in the family, for he had it in mind to invade Louis the Eleventh's kingdom.

When Henry the Fifth had died the lands won by him had been lost during the reign of Henry the Sixth, Edward's predecessor, and the English people, remembering Agincourt, burned to regain them from the hated French. So to this end he persuaded Parliament to grant him sums of money and called upon his subjects to help towards the raising of a great army.

These contributions were called 'benevolences' and Elizabeth of York found herself riding beside her father as he showed himself to his subjects, encouraging their generosity.

'How proud I am of my glorious father,' thought the nine-year-old girl. Edward was now in the full flower of his manhood, adored by his people, Warwick his one-time friend and later enemy dead, his two brothers temporarily quietened.

He rode through the streets of his capital between the houses of the London merchants interspersed with humbler dwellings, the large gardens of the former making a welcome 'breathing' space in the crowded streets where the people jostled one another to see their King with his colourful escort ride by.

She saw how the women of the town pressed full purses into his hand, reaching up to touch his sleeve or knee as he went by, and from the windows the merchant's wives leaned out to watch and augment the growing hoard.

One elderly dame, richly clad, even caused her servants to make a way for her through the crowd with their staves in order to reach him and handed up a bulging bag of clinking coins. Elizabeth saw how her father bent down from his horse to accept it, dropping a kiss upon the lady's wrinkled brow. In high delight she called out gleefully, 'for the sweetness of thy breath thou shalt have more' and from the pouch at her girdle pressed even more gold into his willing palm.

So, encouraged by their King's personality, the people responded nobly, especially the women, who were enchanted at his handsome presence, and his daughter rode back with him to the palace. She heard her mother speaking ironically to him.

'The women of our country agree with the ladies of the court that my husband is one who loves their sex,' and his good-natured answer,

'Why should I not accept that which they are so anxious to bestow. Surely my name of 'benevolence' gives greater results than a law with its 'give or else I take' which could cause them anger.'

Elizabeth knew that he had sent to her Uncles George and Richard and they, too, had promised men-at-arms to ride under their standards with the King. Edward had also enlisted the aid of the Duke of Burgundy, the husband of his sister Margaret, to partner him in his undertaking and Charles had promised his support, so the night before the company set off for the Kentish coast, where they were to embark, Edward gave a great banquet to celebrate the expedition.

The atmosphere in the great hall was alive with excitement and expectation. The knowledge that Louis had no desire to meet the English in battle had encouraged the spirits of Edward and his commanders, but Elizabeth in her customary place on the King's left hand was apprehensive. She pressed herself against the side of the beloved figure and he turned to smile at her.

'What do you fear, my daughter,' he said, sensing her anxiety.

Her eyes searched his face.

'You go to war. Many are killed, even kings. I have doubts about your safety.'

He squeezed her hand reassuringly.

'I have many to fight for me and your Aunt Margaret's husband awaits us at Calais. Put away your dread. I have some great position in mind for you when I have beaten Louis.'

Elizabeth pricked up her ears. A great position, what could he mean? But on questioning him he only laughed,

'Let me finish this business first. When I return I will tell you of it,' he promised.

So the following dawn in early July the great army set sail. Men-at-arms, archers, artillery, all were loaded on to the ships and they disappeared into the early morning mists.

But once disembarked at Calais the King received a shock: there was no sign of the Duke of Burgundy and the troops had perforce to wait until he arrived.

On the second day however, Margaret, his Duchess, rode in to welcome her three brothers. She brought gifts for them and her eyes scanned the three waiting figures backed by their entourage.

It was many years since she had left England to marry the Duke in 1468 and she gazed at Edward with delight, then turned to welcome her favourite brother George, who assisted her to dismount. Her eyes turned to the third figure and recognition came.

'It is my little brother Dickon' she said joyfully. 'Time has made you a man.'

She gestured arrogantly to her attendants, her eyes sparkling, her colour high,

'Bring gifts for my beloved brothers,' she ordered.

First, a golden box, its lid encrusted with rubies for Edward, then for George a cloak of velvet trimmed with gold, its lining of lamb's-wool, and for Richard a silver dagger in a pearl-encrusted sheath. There were also brooches for their cloaks and hats and rings in filigree settings for their fingers. Much laughter resounded as the latter were tried on and Richard's were found to be too small.

'I still think of you as a small boy,' she chaffed, 'but you are a soldier now.'

It had been a happy reunion though overclouded by the non-arrival of

Charles, and eventually Clarence and Gloucester escorted their sister back to St Omer, where they waited for word from her husband.

The Duke, however, true to his nickname of 'The Rash' had decided in his erratic mind to besiege the unimportant city of Neuss and when finally he turned up in Calais it was with only a small bodyguard. Airily he informed Edward that he was sure the English King was capable of sweeping across Normandy, subduing it, and meeting Charles himself at Neuss.

But Edward had now lost all faith in his brother-in-law, for when Burgundy departed to rejoin his Duchess, the King learned that Louis had advanced to Compiègne with a formidable army.

So he sent a messenger to Louis, enquiring as to his desire for peace, and the French King was quick to respond.

Backwards and forwards rode the ambassadors, and finally Edward called a council of his commanders, the Dukes of Clarence and Gloucester, who had returned to Calais, the Dukes of Norfolk and Suffolk. The Queen's son by her first marriage the Marquis of Dorset, the Earls of Northumberland and Pembroke, and Rivers her brother. Many crowded into the tent and agreed to accept the proposals of the French King, but then the quiet voice of Richard of Gloucester spoke from amongst them. He moved forward,

'I oppose this,' he said.

Edward stared at the slight figure in its corselet of steel.

'Dickon, this is not like you to go against my wishes,' he said.

Richard's face was flushed but he went on steadily,

'My brother, the English people have given much of their gold towards this war. What will be their reaction to such news?'

Edward regarded his brother thoughtfully,

'Richard, without the help of Burgundy I am not confident of victory. Now he has shown himself but a poor brother-in-arms and one not to be relied on. The treaty that Louis proposes is one of advantage to both sides and one I know he will keep for very fear lest I resume the war.'

Richard's voice was obstinate.

'We are committed to fight! Nothing can alter that.'

Edward sighed, turning away.

'I do not agree with you. My commanders understand my reasons and it must be so.'

So for the first and only time the watching nobles saw division between the King and his younger brother but time showed that it led to no lessening in the regard between the two.

It was on August the fifteenth that the ambassadors of the two sides finally met, the English riding to the little village of Picquigny, and there on a bridge over the river Somme the two Kings met.

Edward was superb in cloth of gold and a velvet cap but Louis was a shabby figure in black as they advanced to a wooden barrier, embraced through the bars and signed the treaty. Behind the English King stood his brother Clarence, but Louis noted the absence of the Duke of Gloucester.

In the following days Louis entertained the English at Amiens and, although Richard accepted the customary courtesy gifts of plate and horses, there was little amity between himself and the French King and ever afterwards Louis' mind listed Gloucester as an enemy of his country.

Back in England Elizabeth of York had waited in trepidation and she received the news of the treaty with delight. The anger of the English people that Richard had predicted caused her no alarm. Her father was safe and she prepared to welcome him home with all the love of her tender heart. So she waited until later that evening when she sat with her parents in the Queen's apartment overlooking the river at Greenwich.

Her small brothers and sisters, worn

out by the excitement of the reunion had been carried off by their attendants, and Elizabeth fixed anxious eyes on her father.

Edward surveyed his Queen, a little smile playing about his lips. Absence had heightened desire and he was conscious of the need to retire to her bedchamber and enjoy that still beautiful body. But he was conscious of his daughter's impatience and he turned to her teasingly,

'Would you know the clauses of the treaty which has given me such satisfaction? Louis has agreed to pay me seventy thousand crowns and fifty thousand a year thereafter' — he paused and the solemn eyes of the young girl stared back at him. What was this to do with her, she wondered and burst out suddenly,

'My father, tell me what you know I am so anxious to hear. That which you promised me before you went overseas.'

He took the young face between his hands, one finger tracing the beautifully moulded nose and sensitive lips,

'It gives me much pleasure to think that one day you may be Queen of France,' then before she could speak again went on,

'I expected to return to England victorious but it was not to be. Instead, this treaty suits both the King of France and myself. Amongst its clauses I have already mentioned is one that I will marry my eldest daughter to the Dauphin of France. Surely that means my little Elizabeth. You are my eldest daughter, are you not, my sweeting? Therefore it seems that in the fullness of time you will wear a crown.'

Elizabeth stared back at him. It was a bewildering aspect that his words held out. A Queen like her mother, who was married to the handsomest most understanding man on earth. Her eyes brightened and she spoke eagerly,

'Tell me of the Dauphin. Is he as fine a man as you?'

Her mother's voice broke in tinged with sarcasm,

'How could the son of the King of France equal the King of England? Nevertheless, he will doubtless do well enough.'

Over the head of their daughter their eyes met and clashed, then Edward spoke lightly,

'You will make a lovesome Queen, my daughter,' and stooped to kiss her lovingly on the brow.

Later, after her ladies had disrobed her, Elizabeth lay in her rich bed watching the shadows lengthen in the chamber as the September sun gave way to the night and thought dreamily of the Dauphin, her future husband. Gradually she drifted into sleep and childish dreams wherein she wore a crown.

On the twenty-second of December the Duke of Clarence, who, despite his faults, loved his Isabel, was shattered by her death in childbirth. She left two children, Margaret and Edward, and shortly after her burial Charles of Burgundy followed her to the grave.

One day George was sent for by the King in private meeting and sulkily he took his way through the corridors of Windsor Castle. His behaviour had deteriorated since the death of his wife and he expected to receive a rebuke for his unpleasant manners about the court, but one look at Edward's face told him that the matter was far more serious.

As he entered the chamber the king turned from his pacing.

'Do you know what this is?' he demanded holding up a letter.

George had a good idea of its contents and his face grew pale as he protested truculently,

'How can I, without reading it?'

Edward's face grew congested.

'I think you know very well. It is from our sister Margaret now through the death of her husband Dowager Duchess of Burgundy. She tells me that she has lately been communicating with you about a certain matter. Now your wife is gone she urges you should marry her late husband's daughter Mary and that you have shown your willingness to do so. By what right have you agreed to do this without first consulting me?'

George showed his arrogance.

'I have a perfect right to marry my sister's stepdaughter should I wish to do so.'

The colour receded from Edward's face and he drew a deep breath, striving to contain his anger.

'You doubtless realise that Mary is heiress of Burgundy and as her husband you would hold great power. What makes you think that I would allow it after your past involvement with the Earl of Warwick when I pardoned your misdemeanours at that time.'

George stared defiantly.

'If your mind works that way, my brother, I shall never marry anyone again.'

Edward's voice was grim as he replied,

'I have also received a communication from the French King. He ever loves to cause me uneasiness under the guise of friendship and tells me that Margaret has boasted of the power you will hold. Our sister is always one to poke her finger in any troubled brew. You give me no reason to trust you once you are ruler of Burgundy.'

With a wild gesture Clarence flung himself towards the window of the small room and stood staring out at the river below with its gaily decked craft.

'Louis is a mischief-maker. You prefer to trust him to your own brother?'

Edward's answer was bitter.

'Yes, this brother. I should have no fears of Richard behaving so.'

The sound of that hated name brought George round with flaming countenance.

'There are many who think your own position is not so assured,' he said spitefully.

Now tempers rose high between them and the two brothers faced each other as Edward snarled,

'Do not be mistaken, little brother. I am fully aware of the rumours going about the Court that you say I am no true son of our father's and traduce my mother's name in the saying. Be careful, George, your jealousy drives you too far and I see a bitter end from your plotting. Leave me, and think well of my words.'

Cursing his sister's letter George left and in the next few days his anger grew. It was not alleviated by the knowledge that shortly afterwards James of Scotland wrote suggesting that the brother of the King of England could be affianced to his sister and Edward rejected the suggestion.

It was December and London lay hidden beneath a blanket of fog. At Court an uneasy silence presaged the mutterings of new trouble for the royal family due to the Duke of Clarence's conduct and one night when the King lay beside his Queen in the marriage bed she spoke softly.

'Edward, I must speak to you.'

He muttered drowsily but she shook his arm urgently.

'I would speak of Stillington, Bishop of Bath and Wells.'

He roused himself then surveying her uneasily and she went on,

'I know why you are so troubled by George's behaviour as he strives to cause unrest about the Court. It is that secret which has always lain between us, causing you intense agony of mind as to what he intends to do about it. Shall I mention a certain name, Eleanor Talbot, daughter of the Earl of Shrewsbury. Stillington knows of the marriage ceremony you went through with her and as Bishop has doubtless leaked the secret to your brother. If mouths are not stopped I, your wife, will be but a whore taken outside the marriage-bed and your son will be a bastard, no longer heir to your crown.'

Edward was silent. For once the ruler had no words and the woman beside him continued,

'Your son's future lies in your hands. George thinks of his own elevation to the throne if you die, but he cannot contain his tongue and must always try to cause you distress. You must take steps to muzzle him before he leaks it to the Council. Edward, this means terrible measures must be taken which do not go well with your feeling as a brother, but for the sake of our son it must be so. Once George is silenced you can send Stillington to the Tower. He is a timid spirit and you can release him when he has learnt his lesson.'

So spoke the Queen, but still Edward hesitated as the months went by until one day it came to his ears that his wife, speaking to a member of her household, had wept, saying that if Clarence was allowed to continue in this way she feared her son would never come to the throne.

Edward knew then that he must move, and Elizabeth of York heard with horror of the arrest of her Uncle

George and his imprisonment in the Tower.

It was a subdued Christmas, that one of 1477, overshadowed as it was by Clarence's dreadful position, but, after it was over, Elizabeth took part in a great wedding where her three-year-old brother, Richard, was married to the five-year-old heiress of the House of Norfolk, little Anne Mowbray.

Bravely she joined in the revels but her heart was torn with sorrow for her two little cousins Margaret and Edward now in the care of their grandmother, the Duchess of York. Only a year ago they had suffered the death of their mother and now their father lay in the gloomy Tower in deadly peril.

$\star$ $\star$ $\star$

Queen Elizabeth Woodville sat in her chamber, pondering upon her early life. Although she no longer had the King's love she was the mother of his children, including that of his son and heir

Edward, and she held him with stronger threads than those of mere passion.

She remembered the days when she had lived with her mother at Grafton Regis after her beloved husband's death, days of silent suffering in which time had passed slowly, unrelieved by any happiness. Until that morning which was to open a new chapter in her life and change her whole future.

She had risen early to walk in the garden of her mother's manor house and had paused to stand under a great tree. Before her lay the expanse of winding paths snaking away to the little stream which marked the boundary of her parents' land from that of the forests beyond where deer and boar roamed freely and behind her lay the sleeping house wherein lay her sisters and brothers together with her two small sons by Sir John Grey.

After their father's death at the second battle of St Albans under the Lancastrian banner the victorious

Yorkists had deprived her of his lands, including that beautiful castle of Bradgate where she had known such happiness. She had returned penniless to her mother's home, knowing that the family had become impoverished by their upholding of the Lancastrian cause, and was received lovingly by them.

Jacqueta of Bedford had taken as her second husband Richard Woodville, a simple knight by whom she had conceived Elizabeth herself, six other daughters and five sons, and was also reputed to practise strange acts which smacked of witchcraft.

As Elizabeth stood now on the dew-soaked grass, upright and slim in her flowing black dress, her silver gilt hair falling below her waist unconfined by band or widow's veil, she heard the sound of a single bell tolling. It came from the monastery a mile away, calling the monks to prayer and with it sounded children's voices as her two sons roused by the sun from their slumbers raced from the house to find her.

'Thomas, Dickon.' She had welcomed them gladly to distract her from the sad thoughts assailing her and, seating herself on the trunk of a fallen oak, she watched them as they ran happily about, picking up the loose twigs and throwing them into the water.

She closed her eyes, leaning her chin on her hand, and listened to the sounds of nature around her, the cool murmur of the little stream as it ran over the loose stones, the voices of thrush and blackbird, undeterred by the shouts of her sons, whistling and calling as if in competition, the drone of the honeybee supping clover and kingcups at her feet. Only one sound was discordant, a huntsman's horn brayed but so distantly that it merged into the pleasant symphony around her.

So she rested but soon became aware of the rustle of approaching steps through the forest and raised her head as a great horse with its rider made its way towards her, splashing through the water as it crossed the stream. It was a giant of a man, who, on seeing her, halted his steed while she rose to her feet warily and stood watching him.

As he dismounted she saw he wore a hunting tunic and short cloak of green, his hose was silk, his boots of softest doeskin and she raised her eyes to his face. The skin showed fair, the newly growing beard golden in colour and the bare head showed the hair curling round his ears and neck. He stared back at her, his pose confident and the speedwell blue of his fine eyes struck her with their beauty. As they stood surveying each other the boys ceased their play and came to stand protectively beside her and the seven-year-old Thomas spoke forthrightly,

'Who are you? This is my grand-dame's land. Only those we know as our neighbours frequent it.'

The stranger smiled, showing perfect teeth, and spoke placatingly,

'I ask your pardon, young sir! I have

outdistanced the hunt and lost my way,' and he gestured to the bow and arrows at his hip and the jewelled dagger he wore in his belt.

Elizabeth's mind was busy. She saw the gold trappings of the fine destrier, the flash of precious stones in the rings he wore and noted the arrogance of his manner despite the pleasant way in which he spoke to the boy and suddenly she knew who he was. This was no unknown neighbour she thought as she remembered it was rumoured that the Yorkist King often hunted these parts. Before her undoubtedly stood Edward of March, King of England and she put out a hand to restrain her son.

Instead, it was taken firmly by the newcomer, who spoke reassuringly,

'Do not fear, my lady, you are as safe with me as any neighbour. Come, sit and recover yourself.'

He bent over her as she rested again on the tree-trunk and she smelt the sweetness of his clothes. Her face was burning, her brain afire. This man who stood smiling down at her was an enemy. He had taken everything from her and her family and she stiffened with sudden hatred. He seemed to become aware of her feelings, for he straightened and the smile disappeared. He turned to look again at the boys and his tone now was authoritative,

'I heard your voices and thought you might direct me. What is your name, manikin?'

Resentful at the derisory title the boy answered him sharply,

'Why do you ask? I am Thomas, this is my brother and our mother here is Dame Elizabeth Grey. Our father was Sir John Grey of Groby. He was killed by the Yorkists and we live here now with our grandmother, the Duchess of Bedford.'

Elizabeth felt sick. To speak so to the head of the Yorkist clan, he the child of an avowed traitor, a Lancastrian knight. Shrinkingly she threw a side-long glance but the gaze now turned again upon her showed no sign of anger as he spoke generously.

'Dame, you have a fine son and a true champion of his father. Know you my name?'

His eyes were on her face, a little spark glinting, and she spoke faintly, rising to curtsey uncertainly.

'You are the King.'

He laughed aloud, turning to throw his horse's reins over a nearby thicket, then moved to put a strong hand under her arm,

'Come, that curtsey is not worthy of your King. Save it until you are more composed. Methinks I might be Lucifer himself by your expression. Believe me I am not one to harm a lady and her sons even if her husband was my enemy. A true knight treats his adversary's women folk with courtesy.'

His eyes held admiration as he gazed at her and he went on softly,

'I do not look on you as an antagonist. By God's blood, you are the most beautiful woman I have ever seen. Surely you will allow me to conduct you to your home.'

It was a command not a request and as such must be complied with and as he turned to retrieve his mount her younger son ran forward, his face flushed, his eyes bright,

'Sire, your Grace, may I lead him?' he begged.

The King looked down at the eager face at his elbow.

'What is your name, my stripling?'

'It is Richard,' the boy replied.

Edward's face brightened still more.

'I have a young brother whom I love dearly by that name. For that reason, if not for any other, I grant your request. Catch!' and he tossed the reins to the delighted boy.

So the little party walked back to the house and found it already stirring into life. The few serving folk whom Richard could afford went about their tasks, the nurse in charge of the boys came running to admonish them for their disappearance but paused on seeing the stranger, and Jacqueta and her husband were quickly made aware of the newcomer's identity. The lady made obeisance, her eyes quick to notice his frequent glances at her daughter and as she turned to lead him into the house she spoke submissively,

'Will Your Grace accept refreshment?'

Richard Woodville stood by uncertainly. He knew he had forfeited his few estates and civil rights by this man's advisers and left only this simple manor house in which he lived and he feared Edward's reaction, but the King answered heartily,

'I should be happy to do so, madam.'

While wine and comfits were brought, Elizabeth remembered how he had taken his place in the solar, his easy manners relieving the tension. He spoke of the relaxation he enjoyed in hunting through the forests of Oxfordshire from his old palace at Woodstock, the rising at dawn to feel the new morning's air on his face, the absence of ceremony and protocol as his steed trod the path beneath the spreading trees and, as he talked, Elizabeth saw how his eyes noted the shabbiness of the gowns his hostess and her daughter wore and the poverty of tapestries and furniture.

Soon after, he rose to his feet bowing courteously to his hostess,

'My companions will be searching for me. May I beg one of your retainers to attend me until I find them?' His eyes turned to Elizabeth,

'My lady, I thank you for your courtesy. If I come this way again I trust we shall meet,' and as he rode away accompanied by a groom of the Woodville stable he turned in his saddle to raise a hand in farewell.

Back in the house conversation was excited and apprehensive but Jacqueta drew her daughter into her own chamber.

'My child, what think you of our King. Does he cause you the interest he so obviously feels for you?'

There was a flush on Elizabeth's cheeks as she met her mother's gaze.

'I am well aware of his interest,' she said coldly. 'He is well known for a womaniser, but I have no intention of becoming a vehicle for his lust. He will get no response from me beyond the deference I must extend to a King.'

Her mother spoke angrily.

'The fortunes of our house depend upon his goodwill. Think of your sons and the circumstances in which we live. Now is no time to brood on the past. Our cause is dead and we must turn to the future. It lies in your hands, the recovery of our position and the favour of the new monarchy.'

The days passed and always Jacqueta's voice assailed her,

'You are no virgin. What matter if you give way to the King's passion for you. Surely the return of our lands means more than an hour's dalliance in Edward's arms.'

Her sisters watched curiously. They shivered at the thought of armed men riding to the Manor House and wondered what the King's renewed interest in the Woodville family would bring. They had been allowed to sink back into obscurity after the disgrace of their father. Money was scarce but at least there had been no fear. Now they were conscious of renewed apprehension by Edward's visit and they dreaded his revived memories of their family.

It was a week later that a messenger in the King's livery rode to Grafton Regis and Richard Woodville received him with ashen face. But the news was good. King Edward, it said, had been pleased to grant him a free pardon for his past offences and his daughter Elizabeth's lands through her late husband were to be returned to her with sufficient money for their upkeep. And hot on his heels came the King again, riding with only two or three attendants and once again he walked with Elizabeth and she spoke with downcast eyes and demure looks. But beneath her calm front rebellion flared. If he hoped to win her body by this gift she thought to herself he was wrong.

They paused by the little stream and turning he took her by the arms.

'My lady,' he said thickly and the sweat stood out on his forehead, 'you have not mentioned my message to your father. Does it not please you?'

She smiled. 'Your Grace honours me and I thank you for it.'

He went on roughly.

'You know how I feel for you, Elizabeth. No woman could fail to understand that.'

She pulled herself away and spoke coldly. 'Sire, I pray you let us return to the house.'

Sullenly he followed her and as they went he caught her again by the arm and began to plead with her but although her heart beat fearfully she kept on walking and in vain he stormed and begged until finally as they came in sight of the manor he left her and, after calling to his men, rode away in anger.

A week later he came again and renewed his attack as they sat side by side on that same tree-trunk where they had first met. His voice was hoarse with pleading.

'Bessy, give yourself to me.' She turned away, feeling the heat of his passion in the hands that caressed her and suddenly he shouted at her.

'You bitch, do you realise how you torment me.'

The corner of the widow's veil she wore now whenever they met became entangled in the sleeve of his rich tunic and as he tore it impatiently away it fell on the ground and her hair tumbled about her shoulders. With a frustrated groan he wound his hands in it, burying his face in the perfumed softness and vainly she strove to free herself. He pulled her so that she lost her balance and fell to the ground and as his body covered hers his hands tore at the neck of her gown. In sudden fear she struck out at him and, pulling out the small dagger he wore at his belt, he held it to her throat. Feeling the prick of the sharp blade against her flesh she had remained frozen with horror, staring into the inflamed eyes above her, then she saw the lust die out of his face and with a great sigh he left her, rising to hold out his hand and assist her to her feet. They had walked back to the house together and there he spoke placatingly,

'Forgive me, Bessy. I have never yet taken an unwilling woman,' and took her hand to kiss it gently.

She had ignored her mother's questions after he had gone and kept herself apart from the family but, three days later, from her window she saw him ride in with those who had accompanied him before and when she was sent for and stood before him he said quietly,

'Lady Elizabeth, I would speak with you alone.' Her mother retired and he stood looking down at her, his face strained, his blue eyes pleading.

'Marry me, Bessy,' he begged, 'you shall be my Queen.'

She stood silently, her senses reeling. This was what she desired most of all.

His handsome face and great frame meant nothing to her. All her love was buried in John Grey's tomb, but a great future for herself and her family lay now before her. Queen of England! A wave of triumph swept over her and she put out her hand to him so that he pulled her against his breast. She felt his hot breath as his mouth claimed hers fiercely, but his hands were gentle about her and he did not attempt any lustful movements.

They were married the following morning. Her mother had been told and Jacqueta made her arrangements, failing not to give thanks to that nameless one she believed in. So they were united and her mother entertained the King, giving out that Edward was staying for a few days' relaxation under her roof.

But that evening Elizabeth stood secretly in the bedchamber of the apartments allotted to His Grace, and her mother put on her a silken robe and brushed out the wonderful hair so that it fell like a cloak about her, and whispered in her ear,

'Frustrate not the King in his desires and you will gain power for our family,' and her daughter listened with a little smile playing about her lips. When her mother had gone she stood by the great bed, her mind suddenly alive with memories when as a virgin she had gone to John Grey. She heard the door open and Edward stood there. After that, everything had dissolved in a haze of emotion. No woman could have remained calm or indifferent under the assault of the handsome giant who now possessed her. She was like an unawakened maid under his experienced attack compounded of lust and desire for her alone.

Afterwards as he slept beside her she bit her lips to keep back the sobs. This was not what she thought of as marriage, it was almost rape after the tender carefulness of her first husband and she clenched her hands beneath the coverlet. She would extract every ounce of power for her body's surrender she told herself fiercely.

It was the next day that the King requested the Lady Elizabeth's company and when they were out of sight of the house he spoke to her,

'You are the most beautiful of women, my Betsy, and right worthy to be my Queen. Give me a few days' grace. The Earl of Warwick is even now on his way to France to arrange a marriage between me and Bona of Savoy, the French King's sister-in-law. When he returns, the council will be told that I already have a bride and a Queen. That troubles me not at all.' He put his arms round her and his mouth moved lovingly over her face and throat,

'But there is something, my dearest love, which I must tell you.' His arms tightened and he spoke almost shame-facedly, 'Many years ago when I was but a boy I became affianced to another. She was the daughter of the Earl of Shrewsbury and I but the son of

96

Richard of York with no thought of the throne.'

He felt her stiffen and went on hastily, 'for many years she has been withdrawn into a convent, knowing I had but a callow boy's infatuation for her. We have never met for many years and no one knows of our marriage save the Bishop of Bath and Wells. He is too careful of his own skin to divulge it, knowing I have the power to destroy him.'

Fury engulfed her. She had been trapped. He had not told her until she had relinquished the citadel of her body and what would she gain and how much would she lose if she quarrelled with him now. So she smiled into his face with just the necessary show of regret.

'I am yours, Edward, nothing can alter that.' Her acceptance of his secret, which had troubled him much, gave him great relief. One other only knew of it, his mother Cicely, Duchess of York, but the secret would never be breathed by her for the sake of the good name of the House of York.

Elizabeth waited. The news of her marriage broke upon the Court like the crackle of lightning in a cloudless sky and she heard of how the Court reacted to it. The Earl of Warwick did not hide his fury and the majority of those at Court whispered and frowned, showing their disgust. Names began to come to her ears, the King's two brothers Clarence and Gloucester, Thomas Earl of Desmond, Lord Hastings the King's crony and voyeur, and she stored them away in her mind for future reference. The Court muttered viciously, 'Our Queen is a Lancastrian' — to what ends would Edward go to slake his lust, they asked. Many women of the Court in whose arms he had lain wondered why they were not holding the position now themselves instead of a traitor's widow. But Edward ignored them and eventually the whispering died down.

So she had ridden to London with her parents and two small sons and was housed in Westminster Palace. She saw the haughty Earl of Warwick bow the knee to her at the coronation ceremony, felt the anointed crown rest upon her head, walked surrounded by richly dressed courtiers all waiting upon her pleasure. Power was a heady emotion, she learned, and gloried in it. Step by step, she watched the highest in the land salute her with lowered gaze and pursed lips and saw her ladies rush trembling to satisfy any desire she expressed. As she sat at meat many an earlier look of dislike or hauteur from some proud dame was now repaid a hundredfold as the woman stood with aching back and limbs as their new mistress picked delicately at the trencher before her or eyed them malevolently over the ruby-studded cup from which she drank. Even her mother had stood faint and weary for daring in the past to have suggested that her daughter should become the King's mistress.

Now the Court centred on her, and

the Woodville family challenged the rule of the older nobles. Many rich positions fell to her brother and sisters, and to her father came the title of Earl Rivers to be followed by the high office of Constable of England.

She had proved fruitful too, giving birth in quick succession to two daughters. It was just before the third child was born that she was stirred to bitterness again. One of her ladies spoke apart to the others in the Queen's chamber as Elizabeth watched from behind lowered lids, her white hands busy with her embroidery needle; she saw how they gathered together like gaily coloured flowers shaken by a passing breeze as they listened.

She spoke in icy tones, 'Come here,' and her manner was an offence to their pride. Slowly they obeyed, sullen faces regarding her from beneath the butter-fly headdresses, and her words were tipped with acid. 'Of what do you speak? Methinks it causes you much amusement.'

Silently they surveyed one another, and she sensed their fear as a voice spoke tremulously,

'It is nothing, Your Grace. Just some gossip not fit for your ears.'

Her answer came like the crack of a whip.

'Answer me quickly, girl, or you will suffer.'

The daughter of an earl cringed like a frightened hound but her blood gave her the courage to speak uneasily.

'His Grace rode one day with the Earl of Desmond, home from Ireland, and the King was heard to ask a question.

''What think you of my marriage, Thomas?'

'Desmond shrugged his shoulders.

''It is not my place to comment on such a thing to my liege.'

'The King said forcibly,

''Answer me, Desmond, what think you of my Queen?'

'The answer was given reluctantly, 'Your Grace, the Queen is very beautiful but not worthy of such high position. It would have pleased many if you had married a foreign princess.' The King had but laughed and clapped the other upon the shoulder and they rode off together.'

Shortly afterwards Edward had set out on progress to the south of his kingdom and the Queen knew she was again with child. The bile rose in her throat each morning but it was a small discomfort beside the rage which tore at her when she thought of the words of the Earl of Desmond.

'Not worthy of her place.' Each morning as the sickness assailed her she recalled how she repeated the words in her mind and, as the days passed, the hatred for the man who had voiced them lay like the dregs of wine at the bottom of a cup. She knew with Edward absent she held command and one day, secretly, she sent for the Great Seal, dictating the words of a certain document to a trembling clerk. One word leaped out at her from the page

— 'treason' — and as she went to sign her name her mother, standing beside her, spoke. 'Elizabeth, there is something you have forgotten.'

She met her daughter's gaze and smiled. 'This Desmond has two sons who may live to avenge their father's death. Kill the tree at its roots, my daughter. So are your own made safe.'

With steady hands the names were added. 'This for my children's sake,' she muttered, and her signature stood full and bold beneath.

As she returned to her chamber drained of all emotion she felt the four-month-old child stir in her womb and whispered to herself, 'No one shall live to cause you care, my son.' But it was a girl who was born before Edward reached home in good spirits.

Elizabeth remembered now how she had greeted him and ordered a private meal in her own apartments, perfuming the great bed and arranging herself in a rich cloak of velvet and fur, but he was long in coming. At last, though, she had heard the sound of the guards' weapons saluting him outside the door and he came into the room quickly. But the door rattled with the force of its closure and his eyes were like blue flame as they went over her slim form, his head lowered like a charging bull's.

She spoke falteringly, 'Edward,' and his voice came back to her as if strangled in his throat.

'What is this I am told?'

She feigned ignorance.

'What are you told?'

Speaking almost in a whisper he raised clenched hands above his head.

'Desmond, the man who lay in my bosom, my friend, my Lieutenant of Ireland! You destroyed him. The Great Seal to which you had no right you stole and signed his death warrant. Your name is there for all to see — my Queen's name. Tell me,' and his voice which had slowly risen ended in a shout. 'Tell me what did he do to deserve this?'

Fear for herself was overlaid by the

dead man's remembered words and she spat out viciously,

'He traduced me — said I was not worthy to be your wife. I, the mother of your babies,' and she repeated the dead man's words.

But there was no lightening of the King's anger save that he moved closer to her.

'And what of his children. Did they also sully your name. What fiend possessed you to make them suffer?' Grasping her arms he shook her until her head spun, then pushed her away so that she fell against the bed and she barely heard his muttered words.

'If you ever bear me a son, God grant no man treats him as you have just treated Lady Desmond's,' and he turned to leave. She sprang after him, catching at his sleeve.

'I love you, Edward. The thought of not being worthy tears me apart.'

He had looked down at her from his great height and she saw the mark of tears on his face.

'Methinks it is a strange sort of love that takes pleasure in deception. My mind now explores other possibilities. You are wonderous fair but I have noticed lately a coolness in our mating which speaks not of true affection. Also I have not yet a son so necessary to every king.'

Looking back over the years she remembered the little chill that had touched her at his words as he left, she wondered if she had leaned too heavily upon his desire for her. Now that his first passion was assuaged he had become aware of her sexual ability and knew it to be lacking in true fervour so he had turned to other women.

She knew now that he sought her bed only occasionally, as ladies at Court provided him with the stimulations he needed in his sexual pursuits and also the wives of the great merchants anxious to lie in the King's arms.

She burned at first but grew gradually to ignore his infidelities and so the years had gone on until Warwick's defection and Edward had hurried his family into the Tower. But the night before he left he caressed her with more true affection than he had showed for some time.

'God knows how things will befall, Bessy,' his hands stroked her hair in the way they had done before the tragedy of Desmond. 'Remember the child you carry. If it is a boy, as my heir it will be the focus of many ambitious men. Do not forget that George even now fights with Warwick against me and trust him not. Remember that other, but a boy, who will be loyal I know — Richard my young brother whom I love dearly.'

So the next morning he had ridden away and all those terrible days in sanctuary had followed until his triumphant return.

So Elizabeth the Queen sitting in her chamber reviewed her past life and realised that with the incarceration of the Duke of Clarence in the Tower her whole life trembled upon the knife-edge of disaster. What she and the King had hidden for so long might now be a secret no more. Elizabeth's heart turned over. She could see herself cut off unwanted, her children branded illegitimate, her Woodville family divested of position and wealth. Surely Edward would not let that happen.

When she had begged her husband to eliminate his brother she had imagined arrest followed by imprisonment in the Tower and swift execution, not this public trial wherein the two faced each other in a crowded courtroom where George might take it into his head to spill the dreadful information in public. And then suddenly it was all over, the terror, the agony of mind was as if it had never been.

The snow fell heavily following the wedding of the King's younger son to Anne Mowbray and the people took to the frozen ponds to skate on bones fashioned to their shoes, their cheerful voices ringing out on the wintry air. But the King strode about the Court with troubled looks. Repeatedly he spoke with his brother Richard, who had ridden to London for the wedding, and their conversation centred on the coming trial of their brother George.

One day from a window of the Queen's chamber in the palace Elizabeth saw a small procession riding back from the Tower and watched her father and uncle disappear into the courtyard below.

Elizabeth Woodville had joined her at the window, turning to dismiss her ladies peremptorily, and then stood waiting. Her daughter was troubled. She felt the tension in her mother's bearing, saw the look of apprehension in her eyes and felt anxiety rise in her own breast.

The door opened and Edward stood on the threshold, behind him Richard of Gloucester, and his expression was terrible in its misery.

'It is over,' he said. 'George has been sentenced to death and it is my command which must take his life.'

His wife did not speak. She stood

with expressionless gaze as she faced her husband, only in the proud tilt of her head and relaxed hands half hidden in her robes did she show the triumph that his words brought her. The knowledge that she had won a battle was very obvious to her daughter.

The King's eyes were on her and for a moment it seemed he would break into reproachful speech but he turned on his heel, pushing past his brother and quit the room. The Queen followed him and Elizabeth stood hands clasped to her breast, the tears beginning to roll down her cheeks. It was Gloucester who closed the door, coming towards her with outstretched arms and she went into his embrace, burying her face in his velvet tunic.

He held her closely while she sobbed out her misery but finally he spoke gently:

'I feel as you do, Elizabeth, but such relief comes not to men. Try not to show such distress, your father has enough to bear.'

She raised her head, looking up into the thin face with the marks of the past week's trouble upon it.

'Uncle Richard, you, too, must have suffered much.'

He answered her bitterly.

'My pleas to your father have brought no response. My heart is filled with grief at the sentence. But you, little maid, are too young to be made unhappy by these tragic events. You must put it out of your mind.'

He took her face between his hands, kissing her tenderly, his mouth on her brow. In an excess of feeling she clung to him.

'Oh, Uncle Richard, I love you,' she said.

He smiled then, standing back to hold her hands in his,

'As I love you, sweetheart. As my dearest niece you are very close to my heart. Remember to give that understanding and love to your father especially at this time.'

She watched him as he left the room

and was conscious of some new unexplained emotion in her heart which she did not understand. As the days went on it grew stronger and she became aware of a desire within her which longed to see him again.

A week later the King steeled himself and the sentence on George, Duke of Clarence, was carried out.

Not long afterwards another prisoner took up his sojourn in the Tower for 'Uttering words prejudicial to the King and State' and the Bishop of Bath and Wells pondered regretfully upon his past mistakes.

He wished desperately that he had not spoken so freely to the Duke of Clarence about a certain matter and knew he stood now in great danger. Unfortunately, his diocese had lain in the lands held under the Duke's jurisdiction and one day he had leaked information which he wished now he had left unsaid.

To his intense relief however, three months after, a royal pardon arrived and the Bishop found himself released from the Tower but the poorer by several hundred crowns.

The country recovered slowly from the news of Clarence's execution. He had been extinguished in a butt of malmsey, so it was rumoured, but Edward gave no denial or affirmation of this.

In the following months Elizabeth waited for fresh news of her betrothal to the Dauphin but Louis remained obstinately silent and the trouble with Clarence had held completion in abeyance, but the young girl was very conscious of it and as time went on she grew to realise that her feelings had changed. She no longer thought as a child and was now very conscious of the bitter-sweet joy that the name of Richard of Gloucester evoked.

He had returned to Middleham before George's execution and she did not see him again until Margaret, Duchess of Burgundy, returned to England in 1480 to visit her family, and to celebrate her visit there were many events arranged. Elizabeth was now fourteen years of age, tall, fair with blue eyes and stunningly beautiful features. She revelled in the tournaments and masques which took place together with visits to the Duchess of York, who rejoiced to see her daughter again after twelve years.

Despite the Dowager Duchess's interference in his affairs Edward greeted her lovingly and she for her part tried to forget the death of Clarence her favourite brother. Her stepdaughter Mary was now married to Maximilian of Germany so the young girl's future was settled and Margaret prepared to enjoy the celebrations that Edward had arranged for her.

She sat with her mother Cicely in a pavilion overlooking the tilt-yard, watching a great joust. The sun blazed down on men in polished armour and horses caparisoned in the colours of their riders, on squires and grooms wearing on their breasts the insignia of their masters, but she, her mother, and the many ladies attending them were well protected from the glare by the rich canopy which shaded them.

So many strange faces, so many new emblems she thought, and craved her mother's assistance in identifying them. There went the Marquis of Dorset, Elizabeth Woodville's son by her first marriage. He had been but a boy when she left England, now he was a man riding to take part in the tournament together with the five brothers of the Queen and her younger son, Richard.

The Queen herself was all that she had been told of by her late husband's ambassador, but her beauty was marred by her cold, distant manner and Margaret spoke forthrightly to the Duke of Gloucester.

'Our sister-in-law's behaviour does not please me. She may be Queen of England but I am the sister of the King and Dowager of Burgundy. Her lineage is poor and gives no reason for this high-handed manner. Her father was but a son of the chamberlain to the Duke of Bedford, her mother's first husband, and yet Edward encourages her. I am forced to stand while she takes meat and expected to make constant obeisance to her during the dancing.'

Richard of Gloucester frowned expressively.

'I have no love for the Woodvilles. Let us forget them with their exaggerated ideas of their own importance. You are here to enjoy yourself. Let not your pleasure be marred. I am sure,' and he smiled at his sister, 'you are well able to match her in regality.'

So the Queen and the Duchess of Burgundy lived their days during the latter's visit in a state of mutual dislike, their tongues edged with malice and the Court found much amusement in the clashes between the two women.

Meanwhile Elizabeth of York waited impatiently but was not able to speak with her uncle until a great feast was held in Baynard's Castle and she met him alone in a corridor as she made her way to the great hall.

He greeted her warmly, clasping her hands in his and smiling into her eyes.

'My niece grows more beautiful than ever. You are now fourteen years of age, two years younger than your Aunt Anne when I married her. I am glad that by all accounts Picquigny will come to nothing! Your father must retain you several more years before you are betrothed again.'

Elizabeth's spirits fell. Why did he have to mention his wife and how could he speak so blithely of her own betrothal to another.

'I do not wish to leave England and those I love for another country,' she said passionately.

Richard regarded the stormy face quizzically, 'You are a princess, sweetheart, and will learn to care for the man chosen for you.'

She felt the tears come into her eyes as she spoke recklessly. 'I love another, Uncle Richard.'

Gloucester's smile disappeared but he spoke comfortingly.

'Elizabeth, you know full well you must be betrothed to someone whom your father chooses. It must always be so in your position.'

Forgetting everything but the need for justification of her feelings she burst out, 'You married where you loved.'

He answered her quietly.

'You speak truly, my niece. But I am not a woman and therefore a counter in diplomacy. Neither am I the heir to the throne. When your brother Edward comes to be affianced it will be to some great princess of a foreign house, and he will doubtless come to love her. Remember, too, that your Aunt Anne is of a great house herself and my position is strengthened by my marriage with her.'

Elizabeth winced inwardly as he spoke again of his wife but she persisted.

'If Aunt Anne had been of no great

lineage would you have wanted her?'
she asked.

Face to face they regarded each
other, uncle and niece and after a
moment he spoke thoughtfully,

'I should have loved Anne had
she been but a cook maid. Come,
Elizabeth, let us join your father.'

She held back looking up at him
piteously,

'But the one I love is no scullion — I
will tell . . . '

He broke in on her words, laying a
restraining finger upon her lips.

'No more, little maid. Tis better that
I do not hear his name, only tell me
— does he know?'

She shook her head dumbly and he
smiled in a satisfied manner.

'It is better so, sweeting,' he said.

She allowed herself to be led away
then to the celebrations, but Elizabeth
of York continued to suffer the pangs of
adolescent love for her Uncle Richard,
Duke of Gloucester.

★ ★ ★

Cicely, Duchess of York, from her home in Baynard's Castle watched with dismay the moral and physical decline of her eldest son.

Edward, as the months went on, seemed always more conscious of the terrible fratricidal crime he had committed against his family when he took the life of the Duke of Clarence and had been known upon occasions, while in his cups, to cry that 'No man would make request for this unfortunate brother's life.'

He forgot the constant importunings of Richard of Gloucester, crying thus in self-justification of his own actions and turned to the appetites of the flesh to dull his conscience.

Cicely saw the once splendid King, alert of mind, athletic of body, degenerating into lechery, drunkenness and gluttony, and suffered continual unhappiness as a result. She saw too that her daughter-in-law, whom she had never loved, seemed indifferent to this change in her husband and looked to the possibility of more power as she drew closer together the bond between herself and the members of her Woodville family. Therefore, the two sections of the court, the Woodvilles, and the old nobility found an ever-increasing barrier of divided loyalties and personal dislike sundering them.

Elizabeth, too, was aware of this change in her beloved father and grew to realise that the many fascinating women who surrounded him were harlots whom he enjoyed. Elizabeth Lucy of the cat-like eyes and seductive body was one of many who shared his bed, but his daughter grew to know and tolerate Jane Shore, who had given up her husband to live in the palace and seemed to be trusted by Edward.

'Many women he had but she he loves,' it was whispered about the court.

It seemed to the Princess at this time her life was passing through a trying period. She had known great relief as time went on and there was no more reference made to her marriage with the Dauphin but it always remained as a possibility to be feared.

One day, returning from his duties in the council chamber, the King made his way to his wife's solar, throwing himself down upon a cushioned seat to survey his family with a jaundiced eye. His spirits were low, for the quarrel which had erupted into war between Scotland and England was causing him intense self-pity. His precarious health had made him unfit for campaigning and he relied upon his brother Gloucester to take command of his armies. The knowledge that he could not lead them himself irritated him and he was in no mood for conciliation. His head throbbed from the excesses of the night before, when he had drunk too much of the potent wine, and he moved uncomfortably as he looked at his family.

The Queen and her ladies sat by a window overlooking the privy garden and he watched for a moment their white fingers working busily on the embroidery of the material in their laps. These in time he knew would become altar cloths for the Chapel and hangings for the bedchambers of the palace. Slightly apart sat his eldest daughter her head bent over a copy of *The Golden Legend* from Caxton's press.

The King spoke sourly:

'Elizabeth, your future is continually in my mind. You must be affianced again. Louis of France has no intention of implementing the marriage and we must look elsewhere for a bridegroom for you.'

The girl's hands trembled as she closed the book, her gaze on her father's face.

'I have no desire to leave my country,' she faltered. He threw out his hand, then winced as nausea struck him.

'Forget your desires, my daughter. Every girl child must be a pawn in the game between kings. Much as we love you, understand that your destiny is to tighten the bonds between some foreign country and England.'

Elizabeth stared back at him, remembering that other who had spoken similar words and something in her face touched the King. He rose to his feet, his increasing girth troubling him as he moved towards her.

'Sweetheart, I would not be cruel but I must think continually of the future of yourself and your sisters. Many things worry me. One day your brother will be King. He is but eleven years of age and holds his court in Ludlow with his Uncle Anthony.'

He paused to survey his wife, his look disapproving, 'It is in my mind to bring him back to live under my personal control.'

Elizabeth Woodville raised her head, her chin tilted upwards.

'Why do that, my husband,' she asked coldly. 'Anthony keeps a fine court there. He sees that our son is disciplined in everything which befits a future monarch. In religious exercise, in foreign tongues, in the use of sword and axe and in chivalric tournaments and jousts. Reports come back to you that he grows every day in scholarly attainments and all things which are necessary for him to know as a future sovereign.'

The King met her eyes squarely.

'I fear not for my son's teaching. It is those who oversee him, madam, who cause me concern.'

The Queen's face hardened as he went on: 'He is wholly at the mercy of your family. Your brother, your son Richard Grey, and the aged chamberlain Thomas Vaughan, also the men who give them allegiance. My mind would be more at rest if he lived here under my eye.'

The Queen's fingers tightened on the needle she held but she spoke with restraint.

'You must do as you think fit, Edward, but you show great discourtesy to my family.'

He laughed harshly. 'Your family have shown great disrespect to the older members of my court. I have been overpatient with them and feel it is now time to rectify matters.'

He fell silent then, conscious of the ears which avidly listened to the conversation, though the ladies' heads were bent industriously over their work. He turned away then without more words, and departed from the chamber, leaving behind a shaken daughter and a Queen stirred into resentment against him.

The Christmas of 1482 was one that Elizabeth would always remember. With her sisters she graced the Court as it celebrated the holy feast and knew herself to be the object of much attention as noble lords and their ladies congregated about their King and Queen, dancing and feasting in the Palace of Westminster.

Her sister Cicely was shortly to be affianced to James the Third of Scotland, who was still a minor and much ruled by favourites, and she began to put on the airs and graces of a future consort but Elizabeth ignored her manners. Her rejection by the Dauphin, although causing much animosity between her father and the French king, was a matter of great relief to her, suffering as she did from the ache in her heart whenever she thought of her Uncle Richard.

She found love was a painful emotion. Every mention of his name set her heart beating faster and even as she danced and made merry she wished desperately that he could have been present to share the celebrations with her.

But he had been far away in his castle of Middleham with the woman Elizabeth thought of only as a distant memory. She tried to bring substance to the shadowy figure she had glimpsed that time in Uncle George's household when she was a child and had opened the door where Anne had been kept in strict seclusion. All she could recall was a sad face with blue eyes and hair contained by the now old-fashioned hennin.

It must have been after that when Richard had found and married her. Did he really love her or was it but desire for her lands as Clarence had avowed which made him seek her out? She remembered his thoughtful look and deliberate reply to her question. What a strange answer. 'I should have loved Anne had she been but a cook maid.' What thought had possessed his mind at that time. How could anyone love a cook maid? Anne was the daughter of that great man, the Earl of Warwick. Puzzling over it Elizabeth spoke to Cicely one day.

Their ladies had robed them and they waited to leave their chamber to give their presents for the Christmas feast when Elizabeth broached the subject.

'Uncle Richard is never here to attend the celebrations. I wonder why. Does not his Duchess care for the Court?'

Surveying herself in the steel mirror Cicely shrugged her shoulders.

'I have heard Anne and the little Prince Edward are both sickly in health and he himself has no love for our relatives. They say her health was affected when our Uncle George hid her away in some common tavern so that Uncle Richard could not find her. She suffered much at that time, being treated as a mere scullion. Gossip says that he blames our mother for the death of Uncle George and besides he is too dull to enjoy Court entertainment. He never attends jousts or tournaments save as an onlooker, considering them but a pale travesty of war.'

Despite her seeming indifference Elizabeth felt herself colouring and spoke angrily.

'I do not consider him dull. He is courteous and kind-hearted and I honour him greatly.' Her voice trembled and Cicely turned to look at her curiously.

'Why, Bessy, you speak overgenerously of him. I know our father loves him but they have little now in common. Richard's name is never coupled with any other save his wife's and they say he is ever mindful of her welfare.'

She laid the mirror down and came to look into her sister's face.

'Why do you speak so of him?' she asked mischievously.

Elizabeth turned her face away, the tears starting in her eyes, and Cicely put loving arms around her.

'I am sorry, Bessy. I did not know how you felt for him,' she said regretfully.

They were sent for then and went to take their places with their parents but Elizabeth remained thoughtful. She understood now the strange words her uncle had uttered and her heart was sore. Cicely, also pondering upon their conversation, realised suddenly that her prospective husband James held no such place in her own heart, never having seen him, and when her father and proposed husband quarrelled she felt no regrets when the betrothal was broken off.

★ ★ ★

April, 1483 came in with warm winds and sunshine and one day King Edward called his boon companions to him.

'Come, let us go a-fishing,' he said and they set off through the early morning in high spirits. But as they were rowed down the river in the royal barge, the King's jovial laugh ceased to ring out and he grew strangely silent with no more joking or swearing. Those around him eyed him uneasily and suddenly, to their horror, he staggered and collapsed choking into their arms.

They brought him back to Westminster with stricken faces, past the great cranes loading his ships for trading with foreign ports, to lie in his bedchamber outside the door of which his nobles assembled.

The physicians arrived and took control, plying their skills as they moved quietly about and at first the information coming from the sickroom was encouraging. The King had recovered consciousness. Enormous relief was felt but then a relapse took place and into the chamber crowded the two opposing factions at court.

He looked on those about him and, desperately, through laboured breathing, he begged them to forget their differences and to be true to his little son. But he could see the dissension in their faces and wearily dismissed them.

He turned then to the only man he had trusted all through the years and, sending for the executors of his will made in 1475, he dictated a codicil. It revoked the name of the Queen as Regent and replaced it with that of his beloved brother, Richard, Duke of Gloucester. Then he sent for his children.

Elizabeth gathered together the nine-year-old Richard, Duke of York, her sisters Cicely, Anne, Catherine and Bridget and led them into her father's bedchamber. Against the white pillows his face showed parchment-like and ravaged with sickness, but he held out a shaking hand to them. The younger children fell on their knees, sobbing quietly, but his eyes were turned on the face of his eldest daughter and it was to her he spoke.

'Elizabeth, care for your brother and sisters and be loyal to Edward. He is young to be a king, but your Uncle Richard will watch over his young life until he is old enough to reign.'

His voice broke as he blessed them all, and with a heart full of grief Elizabeth helped the weeping children to their feet and led them away. She was very conscious of a great feeling of loneliness. Her mother had not been asked for, and had made no move to attend her husband's bedside, and as they returned to their private apartments she looked for the Queen.

Elizabeth Woodville was standing with two men, the Marquis of Dorset, her eldest son by her former husband, and her brother, Sir Edward Woodville. At a small table sat a secretary, who, even as the children entered, was hastily finishing a document dictated to him by the Queen.

The Queen saw her daughter's eyes on her and spoke sharply, 'I send a message to your brother at Ludlow,' then turned to her two relatives. 'Thomas, Edward, do what I request of you.'

There was but little sign of grief in her voice and the colour burned in her cheeks. She looked like a woman in the grip of some remorseless ambition, and, bewildered and heartsick, Elizabeth tried to stem the grief of the children beside her.

It was not many hours later that the citizens of London were made aware of the passing of their king and the bells tolled mournfully from the Abbey, St

Paul's and all the churches, and the people poured from the houses down the lanes and byways, gathering in crowds to lament the loss of so beloved a monarch.

The Marquis of Dorset meanwhile, true to the instructions of the Queen, went to the Tower, which he commanded, and seized its treasure while Sir Edward Woodville weighed anchor and left the Thames estuary. Elizabeth Woodville herself, on being informed that her name was expunged from the will as Regent took the other part under her control.

Sadly the funeral ceremony went forward while the Queen waited for the arrival of her little son from Ludlow so that she could have him crowned. Beneath the outward trappings of grief the Court seethed like a muddy pool, its depths stirred by some great convulsion as the Queen encouraged the members of her family to aid her in seizing power.

The Lord Chamberlain, Sir William

Hastings, however, sent two messages secretly to Middleham, where Gloucester resided, the first informing him of the King's death, the other shortly afterwards telling him of the actions of the Queen.

Elizabeth was with her mother as she ordered and counter-ordered feverishly the movement of her family until one day there came a courier racing from the north. He brought with him a letter of condolence for the Queen and a promise by her brother-in-law to be loyal to his nephew. But on the receipt of Hasting's second letter Richard of Gloucester set out to intercept the King's procession, and, at Stony Stratford, arrested Earl Rivers and his party.

In this he was upheld by Henry, Duke of Buckingham, the first peer of the realm, who, on learning the news had left his estates in Brecon, South Wales, and ridden to offer the aid of himself and his supporters to the Protector.

In vain the Queen exhorted the chief

lords of the council to uphold her. The members were growing rapidly more nervous about the situation. They saw in this bid by the Woodvilles to seize power a danger which could have alarming consequence, and they waited for some word from Gloucester.

His actions at Stony Stratford gave them great relief, and, realising that her bid had failed, Elizabeth Woodville cried that she would retire into sanctuary with her family. Every day brought Richard nearer and she feared his arrival in the capital, for she knew her behaviour must have reached his ears.

In great agitation the Queen's attendants laid hands on everything they could, transporting the possessions across to the Abbey and such was the confusion that the packed chests became jammed in the doorway and a great hole had to be ripped in the wall to facilitate the move.

'This must be the worst moment of my life,' thought Elizabeth of York as she sought to comfort her mother. The Queen had collapsed on to the floor of her denuded apartment while round her the younger children raced about in a flurry of activity, picking up and dropping articles, shouting and crying alternately.

Their mother seemed to have lost all control of herself as she tore at her hair until it fell about her shoulders, the tears running down her face. 'My son, my brother, Gloucester has made them prisoner. He will surely do all he can to destroy my family.'

'Mother, Uncle Richard is no murderer.'

Her eldest daughter spoke soothingly, and Rotherham the Archbishop of York, confirmed her words.

'Your Grace, he only does the command of the late King's will. If there is no evil plan conceived your relatives will certainly be released. Be assured no harm will come to them.'

Wearily the Queen allowed herself to be drawn to her feet and, supported by her daughter, she crossed into sanctuary once again, while Elizabeth, but seventeen years of age, devoted herself to the care of her young sisters and brothers. Often she thought of their former occupancy of these rooms, but then her father had been alive and the Queen had not meddled in affairs of the State. Now hope seemed dead and total disaster to have overtaken them.

The Queen by her policy had shown opposition to Richard's appointment as Protector and remained in great fear. She railed repeatedly against her unhappy fate, speaking always with hatred the name of the Duke of Gloucester.

Despite their self-imposed imprisonment there were always many to carry news to the family and in the days that followed they were kept well informed of what went on.

They heard of the arrival of Edward in London, escorted by his Uncle Richard, who gave due deference to the young King, and of the latter's taking up residence in the Tower while preparations were made for his coronation. Also there came a message for the Queen from Gloucester. There was no need for sanctuary he told her, her fears were unfounded.

But the Queen clutched her daughter's arm, speaking distractedly, 'He knows I meant to gain possession of my son before he had been informed of your father's death. I distrust him. We will remain here.'

In her heart she knew that had her efforts been successful she would have taken steps to have the Gloucesters eliminated. She judged Richard's actions by what would have been her own had she won the game.

Through the ensuing days Elizabeth of York heard fresh disturbing news of the postponement of the coronation, of the growing regard of the Protector for Henry, Duke of Buckingham, upon whom many important appointments were bestowed, also of Hastings' growing jealousy as he saw these rewards being heaped upon the Duke, so that he finally withdrew his allegiance.

At the time of Edward's death he had become Jane Shore's protector and now he used his mistress to gain communication with the Queen, who bore no particular ill-will towards her. But it was not long before Gloucester became aware of Hastings' change of heart.

It was during a stormy council meeting in the White Tower that Richard accused him of treason, crying it in a bitter voice, and William Hastings was summarily executed. Bishop Morton, his chief ally, was arrested, and sent under guard to Buckingham's estate in Brecon. Stanley was put under house arrest and Rotherham was sent to the Tower.

Some days later there was a stir outside the Queen's lodging and a little group came to visit her. Crowded into the small, dark room came Bouchier, Archbishop of Canterbury, John, Lord Howard, and several other councillors.

He spoke in kindly tones.

'Your Grace, I am here to beg you to release the little Duke of York into the charge of the Lord Protector. The young King, as you must know, is living in the Tower with many attendants and every comfort. He has horses, dogs, books, to keep him occupied but requires a playmate of his own standing. He repeatedly asks for his brother and the council wish to see the two reunited.'

Elizabeth Woodville turned pale.

'Richard cannot leave his mother. I fear for his health if he is taken out of my charge.'

Canterbury shook his head.

'Do not fear. He will have every care and I myself will see that he stands behind the King in the coronation ceremony.'

A small figure moved forward. In the confined chambers his health had been affected and he looked wan and woebegone. He touched the Queen's skirts imploringly,

'Mother, let me go to Edward. I am not afraid.' He paused as if ashamed. 'We will have a great deal to enjoy together.'

Taking a deep breath the Queen put her arms round the frail child.

'So be it. Take him, Archbishop. But remember that I shall ask for his safe return before God and the world.' Then she knelt beside the boy,

'Farewell, my own sweet son. God keep you in his care,' and she clasped him closely to her.

Through eyes misted with tears Elizabeth of York saw her little brother depart while her mother wept quietly.

Now the Queen began to lean even more heavily upon the daughter whose nature was so much better balanced than her own. Nevertheless, she still sent letters to Dorset and Edward Woodville, who had fled overseas, beseeching them to join the Lancastrians in an attempt to overthrow Richard and return her sons to her.

These letters, with the help of the

Abbot, she smuggled out, but no reply ever came back and Elizabeth watched sadly her mother's furtive scribblings bedewed with frustrated tears. And then the blow which the Queen had feared most fell upon them.

Bishop Stillington, not anxious to have upon his conscience so grave a matter which involved the succession, had given much thought to the secret he had retained for so long. One day he spoke loudly in Gloucester's unwilling ear, and when the content of his revelation became known, Elizabeth, her face white and strained, spoke to her mother.

'Is this true that my father was married to another woman?'

The Queen reviled the Bishop, calling him many evil names, but not once did she deny the accusation of her daughter or strive to give the lie to it. Still her busy brain worked ceaselessly and one day she spoke to the girl.

'I will write again to my son Thomas in Brittany. With him resides Jasper

Tudor and his nephew Henry. This young man, I have heard, hopes that one day he might obtain the throne of England. What finer Queen for him than you my daughter should anything happen to your brothers.'

Henry Tudor! A man whose name she had heard of only in terms of contempt from her father's lips. A poor off shoot of the house of Beaufort, he was the son of the Countess of Richmond by her first marriage to Edmund Tudor. She remained silent. What was the use of arguing with her mother overwhelmed as she was by fears for her two sons.

Then to the further sufferings of the Queen came news of the execution of her brother Earl Rivers, her son Sir Richard Grey, and Sir Thomas Vaughan, all who had been conveyed to Pontefract Castle and there beheaded. On its heels tidings were received that a certain friar, making a speech at St Paul's, had hinted at the bastardy of Elizabeth herself and her brothers and sisters.

If this were so, thought Elizabeth miserably, who now stood in the position of an heir to the throne, she viewed the tangled web of her family's fortunes with ever-increasing fear. In the dark rooms of the sanctuary lived the family of Elizabeth Woodville, bereft of hope, tainted of blood, the Queen's pride and dignity in the dust, cast there by the late King's promises to a woman who had died long ago in a convent.

Then came the greatest shock of all. Richard of Gloucester had consented to accept the crown and, shortly afterwards, they heard the cries and salutations as Richard and Anne went to their crowning. The country had approved the new monarch and the two small boys playing in the Tower were of no account.

With the execution of Hastings and the disgrace of his chief supporter, Bishop Morton, who was there now to give the Queen hope and prop up her cause?

For Elizabeth the time held special misery. The Queen wrapped in the shell of her hatred for Richard, and fears for her sons, sat apart, brooding upon her wrongs while the younger children watched her unhappily whispering the name of Richard as if the new King were Satan himself.

Elizabeth was torn between her family and her feelings for the man who had taken her brother's place upon the throne, and she wondered wretchedly if he felt any regrets for his actions or if his conscience troubled him.

He had now set out on progress through his kingdom and, after York, he turned south to Lincoln, where he received overwhelming news.

Henry, Duke of Buckingham, sated with wealth and honours, had retired to his castle of Breckonbridge in Wales and there, counselled by his so-called prisoner, the wily Bishop Morton, had named Edward as the true King and was riding to overthrow Richard. At the same time a rumour was spreading through London.

For some weeks now there had been no sign of the little princes and gradually through the alleyways, in taverns and public places, the people whispered fearfully, 'The boys have disappeared. They are no longer seen playing in the gardens of the Tower. Where are they?'

The Queen's agony was a fearful thing to watch. She wandered ceaselessly about the chamber, stumbling over anything in her path, oblivious to the clutching hands of her frightened children. She called repeatedly the names of her two sons, 'Edward, Richard, my darlings, my babies,' and in vain her eldest daughter, the tears running down her own face, did her best to comfort her.

As the days wore on, the Queen relapsed into silent suffering, staring hopelessly before her. Her face grew pinched, and sleep evaded her, and, watching this deterioration of her mother, Elizabeth fought to come to terms with her own innermost feelings.

She knew that her uncle's name was now stained by the disappearance of her two brothers and suspicion of him was alive in her mother's breast, and yet how could she accept this? What had Richard to fear from two little boys accepted now as bastards? Why should he sully his name with their murder? There were other claimants to the throne with royal blood flowing in their veins such as John, the son of the Duchess of Suffolk, Richard's sister, and Edward of Warwick, Clarence's boy. Surely her uncle had he been of that mind could have moved against them also?

Long was the time and bitter the thoughts of those in sanctuary until one day the name of Henry Tudor was put forward by the Duke of Buckingham as the new claimant to the throne. With the dropping of Edward's name it surely meant that Buckingham knew the boys were no longer alive, but of the King's involvement in this there was no proof.

No, decided Elizabeth in her own mind, her uncle so kindly, so lacking in any ambition for the crown in the past, was incapable of putting an end to the lives of the nephews whose father he had loved and served for so many years.

The country watched and waited as Richard rode towards Coventry, but eventually heartening news was received. The Duke's revolt had petered out, due to the lack of men to join him and the foul weather he had encountered. Abandoning his troops, he fled and took refuge until one of his servants, for a paltry sum, betrayed him to the King's men. He was taken to Salisbury and there executed.

So Richard returned to London, knowing that the country as a whole stood firmly behind him, while the man in whose name the revolt had taken place remained in Brittany without attempting to set foot on England's shores. The following Christmas, however, encouraged by the Marquis of

Dorset, Henry Tudor stood in the Cathedral of Rennes and swore to marry Elizabeth Plantagenet, thus reuniting the red rose of Lancaster with the house of York.

It was in the following March that Elizabeth sat one day with her mother while the latter perused a letter handed to her by a messenger of the King's household. It was a private letter from her brother-in-law and Elizabeth watching her mother's face saw the emotions of pride and distaste turn into resignation as she read.

Both mother and daughter knew that, a few days before, Richard had appeared before his council, naming the family in the Abbey and had sworn that if they would come out of sanctuary he would see that they were well cared for, would marry the girls to gentlemen born, and give Dame Elizabeth Grey, as he called her, the sum of seven hundred marks annually for her upkeep. He promised also not to give credence to evil reports made about them without enabling them to have lawful defence and answer.

Elizabeth waited until her mother, drawing a deep breath, raised her eyes from the letter and spoke with emotion.

'Your uncle tells me how, to save your brothers from becoming a focus for rebellion, he sent them in Buckingham's charge to Wales, but after the rebellion he could find no trace of them. He states that, had he revealed this, the world would have thought him guilty of their deaths, that Henry Buckingham had caused them to be done away with at his instigation. This he swears is not so. He has no knowledge of what has become of my sons and he tells me this, striving to clear his name to me. He trusts I will keep my council and not reveal it, lest he be further maligned.'

Watched by her daughter she tore the letter into small pieces and spoke tonelessly,

'For the sake of my daughters what can I do but believe him?'

So a few days later the Dame and her children walked into the free air of the City and, added to the relief of the others, was the delight that filled the heart of Elizabeth of York. Her belief in her uncle's innocence had received fresh impetus and, mingled with satisfaction, joy flooded her being as they took horse for the Palace of Westminster.

When they entered the great hall, Richard came to meet them and, as Elizabeth Woodville bent the knee, he, who was now her King, raised her courteously, turning towards his waiting nieces. Elizabeth was conscious of his hands clasping hers and his lips on her cheek and her heart beat rapidly as his grave face broke into a smile.

'Welcome, my niece,' he said and turned to the slight figure standing beside him, 'Here is your Aunt Anne, the Queen, to give you hearty welcome.'

The young girl was conscious of shock. The woman holding out thin hands looked so frail, the unnaturally high colour staining her cheekbones, the rich necklace she wore emphasising the thinness of the neck it encircled, but she smiled sweetly at Elizabeth and spoke cordially.

'Welcome, my dearest Elizabeth. I hope you will give me the happiness of joining my household.'

Thankfully the girl accepted the offer and took up her position as part of the Queen's entourage while her sisters, as Richard had promised, were suitably housed about the Court. Her mother had asked leave and been granted a separate residence, and a certain John Nesfield kept her under easy surveillance.

The atmosphere of the Court was peaceful, with none of the turmoil known during the latter part of her father's reign, and her sisters were happy, but Elizabeth was conscious that a new feeling troubled her.

Brought daily into contact with the Queen she became aware slowly that jealousy assailed her.

What was there in this woman, thought Elizabeth bitterly, to make Richard love her so. Thin, listless, she seemed like a shadow moving about the Court or sitting beside the King at banquets and entertainments, save that no shadow carried with it that hollow cough. But that he loved his wife Elizabeth had no doubts and Anne Neville's presence brought frustration and pain to her.

Meeting the Duke of Norfolk one day as she stood watching the royal couple she saw his critical eye on her and felt the blood mount into her face. She knew he had guessed her secret and hurriedly averted her eyes. With the affection that lay between them she came gradually to feel that John Howard was the only one who might understand her feelings and one day driven to relieve her overburdened heart she wrote a letter to him.

In it she put what she could not say to his face, calling Richard her joy and maker in this world, admitting that she was his in heart and thought and all her future was bound up in him. But still Anne lingered on. Would the Queen never die?

This immature missive she sent by private messenger and Norfolk, after due consideration, put it to one side, but Elizabeth, knowing no relief, wept hopelessly with shame.

She was sitting in the window seat of a corridor one day, watching the comings and goings in the courtyard below, when her uncle passed her, talking earnestly to Thomas Langton, Bishop of St David's. After saluting her with a smile he resumed his conversation, pausing before entering an adjoining room.

Elizabeth knew that the Bishop, together with Dr John Sherwood of Durham, was about to leave to represent England at the Vatican and she resumed her survey of the scene without until a certain name caught her ear. It was that of the Queen and she listened furtively, her hearing alert.

Her uncle was speaking in sad tones. 'As you know, Thomas, my wife is ill and my life is constantly weighed down by it. The physicians apply their remedies with little result but I dare not show my concern lest she is upset.'

He went on and Elizabeth heard his voice shake. 'My wife is every woman to me. She satisfies me as no other could. That is because we understand each other fully, and understanding always nurtures love.'

What words were said after that she did not hear for they moved on, but she sat immobile her sense of humiliation outweighing every other emotion. The memory of the letter, to which the Duke had made no reply, burned in her conscience and she writhed beneath its malevolence. How could she hope after those words spoken about an ailing woman? He evidently saw only with some inward eye and she realised that her feelings showed as but a poor thing beside the passion which burned in her uncle's breast.

In April the Court moved to Cambridge and then on to Nottingham, and Anne seemed to brighten. She spoke hopefully of shortly reaching Middleham, where she would be reunited with her little son.

One late afternoon Elizabeth was on her way to the Queen's chambers and found members of the household crowded before its closed door. It was Alfreda, one of the Queen's ladies, who answered her hasty questions, her face full of sorrow.

'It is grievous news from Middleham. The messenger has just ridden in. The little Prince Edward is dead and the King has come himself to break the news to the Queen.' She went on tearfully, 'Oh, the poor lady! She lost her senses and fell to the floor but we revived her. Alas, that we have to bring her back to so much misery. The King ordered us to leave the room, now we know not what to do.'

There was no sound from beyond the door, no outcry reached them through the stout wood, and all waited, avoiding one another's eyes, while the day drew into twilight. The attendants brought candles and it was Elizabeth with failing heart who eventually moved forward to tap with tentative fingers, and suddenly the door opened and the King stood there.

He stared at the silent crowd his eyes hollow in the blanched face, then his gaze fell on Elizabeth and he spoke harshly, 'Go to her,' he said and stood aside.

She entered the room, and Anne, sitting in a carved chair, watched her, the pale hair falling on her shoulders from the discarded headdress, her face masked in tragedy, and Elizabeth caught her breath in pity as she put gentle arms about the rigid figure. With the help of the ladies she led the Queen into the bedchamber and disrobed her. Anne suffered it silently and only when they tried to lead her to the bed did she push off their comforting hands, crying in tortured tones, 'Leave me alone.'

It was Richard himself who eventually returned, controlling his own grief to put loving arms round her. She looked up into his face, touching it tenderly, 'Edward, our son,' she wailed, and cast herself upon his breast. Tenderly he coaxed her to her feet and she went passively with him to lie on the great bed, staring into space.

A few days later, a sorrowful procession rode first to Middleham then on to Sheriff Hutton for the funeral. It tried the spirits of all concerned as they watched the grief-stricken parents steel themselves to take part in the ceremony, but, although the King maintained an iron control, Anne Neville drooped like a fading flower.

They left the north by short stages and returned to London. Lovingly, the ladies tended Anne and, uncomplainingly, she accepted their ministrations, while Richard turned to the defence of his kingdom. Henry Tudor's name was once again appearing as a menace on the horizon, and the King occupied himself with warning the country of this threat. He sent word to his commissioners in the north, the Midlands and East Anglia to be prepared for invasion, and time went on towards the Christmas of 1484.

Some months before this great festival Elizabeth sat with the Queen and her ladies, many rolls of beautiful cloth spread out before them. Anne's condition seemed to deteriorate continually and her form to become more skeletal while her face fell into the lines of mortal sickness. Continually she tried to hide from her husband and those about her the toll it was taking and, on this occasion, she smiled bravely as she spoke to her niece.

'Elizabeth, come, make your choice for your Christmas robes. Whichever you choose I will wear the same so that all may see that between Queen and Princess there is no difference.'

The girl moved forward reluctantly and Anne fixed her with slightly feverish eyes. As the King entered the room Elizabeth let her eyes rest upon him, savouring the pleasure of his presence, then recollecting those around her she dropped her eyes and moved away. She feared lest the Queen had seen her expression, but Anne made no sign, speaking without apparent constraint to her husband.

Christmas, despite the troubles of the royal pair, was celebrated with great splendour, and the daughters of Dame Grey were richly dressed and suitably entertained.

Only Elizabeth, standing beside the Queen's chair, was conscious of uneasiness. She saw the eyes of many turned upon her and realised that the robes she wore, so like the Queen's in texture and decoration, had become a topic of adverse criticism amongst the courtiers. She was thankful when a messenger came to speak to the King and the watching eyes moved towards the Sovereign. She saw the latter in earnest conversation, then he dismissed the messenger and turned to Francis Lovell beside him. She heard his words spoken with grim satisfaction. 'Henry Tudor has given out that he will invade England this summer. At last I can come to grips with this slippery adversary.'

One day in the New Year the physicians attending the Queen sent word to Richard. They informed him that he must no longer share his wife's bed as her disease was contagious. Bitterly he opposed them but they insisted, pointing out that it was his duty as King to guard his health, and the country would expect him to obey. So eventually he gave in.

Anne lay heavily on Elizabeth's conscience. The painful breathing sounded continually in her ears and, although she was seldom allowed into the chambers where the Queen lay, the air seemed filled with its ghostly whisper.

What right, she began to ask herself, had she to desire Anne's husband? She realised now that he had never made any advances to her either in speech or look beyond the relationship of uncle and niece. Now she could not offer him even comfort, for he seemed almost unaware of her presence.

This was shown her as she waited one morning by the door from whence he sometimes rode in the great park adjacent to Westminster and, as he appeared in dark riding-clothes, accompanied by Francis Lovell his boyhood friend, she moved forward.

He paused, staring bleakly at her, and she spoke hesitantly, 'Uncle Richard.'

A brief smile was accorded her, then alarm struck him. 'The Queen?' he questioned roughly, and she saw the grey colour of fear spread over his features.

Hastily she shook her head. 'The Queen's condition remains unchanged. I do not come from her apartments.'

She watched the colour return to his face as he passed a shaking hand across his brow, then abruptly he bowed his head and turned away.

She stared after him bemused. In that moment she had meant no more to him than an attendant bearing, as he thought, terrible tidings, and when she had reassured him, even his natural courtesy could not hide how little her existence meant to him.

Behind her she heard Lovell's kindly voice. 'Be not hurt, Lady Elizabeth, the King is so heart-stricken that he sees little these days,' and he passed on.

Elizabeth realised now that this anguished man had no part in her life and she endeavoured to face the knowledge bravely.

One day, as she wandered restlessly along the corridor near the Queen's chambers, watching the physicians and sad-faced attendants come and go, she became conscious that the light was failing. It was barely ten o'clock in the morning and as she heard the footsteps of an approaching page she would have questioned him, but he hurried past her in great haste.

Slowly the darkness grew and as it

did so, she saw the King, outpacing his attendants, walk swiftly past. She had a momentary glimpse of his face in the gloom and an icy hand clutched at her heart. She saw him reach the door of Anne's apartments and disappear within while, huddled against the wall, she waited numbly.

Slowly the creeping shadow overwhelmed the sun and, when it passed, Anne Neville, Queen of England, lay dead.

Three days later she was laid to rest in the great Abbey.

★   ★   ★

March drew slowly to its close. The Court was quiet, the King withdrawn into his chamber, brooding on his loss. Elizabeth sat alone one day when her mother came to visit her and spoke softly, 'My daughter, let not your chance slip away. The King is sad and lonely and you can give him comfort.'

Elizabeth looked at her.

'I never see him, he remains alone in his chamber. Besides, he is my uncle.'

Elizabeth Woodville tossed her head.

'The Pope will grant a dispensation. He is always pliant where diplomacy is concerned.'

In halting tones her daughter went on. 'His love for Anne was very great.'

The reply was swift. 'You little fool. In our early days of marriage your father saw no woman but myself. But that passed and many mistresses took my place in his affections. I know that Richard has been true to Anne but now she is gone he will see you in a different light. He will realise that a son of your body will be a greater asset than his sister's boy John, who is now heir to the throne.'

Silence fell between them and presently, watching the girl's face, the Dame laughed softly.

'You speak without words. When he holds you in his arms the thought of Anne Neville will not come between you.'

Elizabeth spoke reluctantly, 'What of Henry Tudor?'

Her mother answered her scornfully, 'He always delays his coming. Even Margaret Beaufort begins to doubt his intentions despite her motherly exhortations to bestir himself to the task. Now Richard may be a better hope for you, my daughter.'

The older woman left then, and Elizabeth, her senses afire, wondered if her mother spoke truly. He was her uncle but only thirteen years older than herself, and the Pope had granted a dispensation to Clarence and his wife, who stood also in the forbidden affinity.

The fact that she would become Queen of England held no place in Elizabeth's calculations. Her heart and mind fixed themselves again upon the thought of being coupled with the man she had adored since her eleventh year, and the prospect of his turning to her in love brought renewed hope to her heart. Her mother's words had opened a joyous future where duty and inclination joined together in a happy partnership. But not for long!

Her grandmother Cicely, Duchess of York, travelling from her self-imposed retreat in Berkhamsted Castle, visited London and after a meeting with her bereaved son, went on to see Elizabeth. She greeted the girl lovingly, noting the bright eyes and hopeful look.

'My dearest grand-daughter,' she said, 'I must warn you against any thought of marriage with my son. You must shortly leave here to find comfort in new surroundings.'

Elizabeth looked at her, the colour fading from her cheeks, 'I do not understand.'

The Duchess spoke urgently.

'There is a rumour going about the Court, put there by your mother, that my son means to marry you and it causes him much concern. He will never take another wife. He told me so himself. The rumour must be contradicted immediately. A meeting of the councillors and chief citizens has been called at his request and tomorrow he will stand in Clerkenwell Hall and repudiate it in public.'

Elizabeth listened in stunned silence, 'It is his will that you travel to Sheriff Hutton, there to live in the household of the council of the north. The Earl of Lincoln and others will join you there.'

So, thought Elizabeth, her heart sinking, this is the end of my hopes. With his public rejection of her she realised that never more could she picture a future as his wife, and her heart was desolate. She put her arms round the other and looked into the wrinkled face.

'Grandmother, what shall I do?' she asked piteously.

A tender smile touched Cicely of York's face. 'It will pass, my dearest. I am an old woman now and have known almost unbearable sorrow. I lost my beloved husband when I was still young. I have seen three sons die and the fourth suffer insupportable grief and turmoil. Time moves on. You are young and I am sure there is a hopeful future for you. Be thankful that you have survived untouched.'

She left then, kissing her granddaughter before she went, and a month later Elizabeth set out for Sheriff Hutton.

Part II

Part II

The Woman

The castle of Sheriff Hutton stood proudly on high ground. Around it lay the deep moat which cut it off from the village, and, not far away to the east, stood the little church which contained the tomb of King Richard's only child, the boy Edward.

The castle itself was old and draughty, with its dark rooms and long corridors, but Elizabeth enjoyed the companionship of those who shared its household with her. Apart from her own ladies, they were John of Lincoln, Richard's heir to the throne, John of Gloucester, his bastard son, and her little cousin Edward, Earl of Warwick, whose father had been executed in the Tower.

It seemed to the nineteen-year-old girl that, in the months since her father's death, one disaster after another had followed, keeping her always in a state of tension, but now living secure in the release of the passion which she had felt for so long for her Uncle Richard she managed to find some comfort in her life.

Her grandmother had been right. In the last three months, time itself had softened the misery his rejection had caused her and she could now think of her uncle without the heart-yearning which, in the past, had caused her so much travail.

She realised why her uncle had sent her away without seeing her again. He dared not give impetus to the wave of speculation which he had striven to kill when he spoke before the citizens in the Hall at Clerkenwell. He had, however, sent her kindly greetings with wishes for her health and well-being and, though she could not speak to him personally, she knew a measure of peace as a result.

The sun rose high and the country-side was bathed in its golden beams as she rode one day through the fields outside Sheriff Hutton accompanied by the little Earl of Warwick. Richard had put no curb upon her freedom and she was able to ride, enjoy the mellow country air, and ponder upon her future. On a pony beside her rode the young son of her late Uncle George, talking in a lively manner and presently they drew rein on a small hillock to survey the peaceful Yorkshire scene about them.

The green-clad moors stretched as far as the eye could see, the slopes of the distant hills merging in tranquil beauty into the purple arch of the horizon, and they dismounted to rest the horses. It was young Edward who broke the silence which had fallen between them.

'My sister Margaret, now in the household of our grandmother of York, says in her letter to me that there has been much movement about the Court and the country. Uncle Richard is now at Nottingham, waiting to hear of

Henry Tudor's arrival from France. He shows great desire to meet the Welshman and settle once and for all this threat to his kingship.'

Elizabeth turned her eyes from the pleasant scene before her.

'How goes it with the people of England?' she asked, 'does Margaret have anything to say about their feelings for this Tudor?'

Edward picked a stone from among the grasses at his feet and tossed it carelessly away.

'She does not mention the people at all, only that our uncle has sent a message to Lord Stanley, commanding him to join him with his followers. Stanley has replied, saying he is ill with the sweating sickness and cannot move yet.'

Thomas, Lord Stanley, was the husband of Lady Margaret Beaufort whose son by her first marriage was Henry Tudor. No wonder, thought the girl, that Richard needed to know where this man's sympathies lay and which way he would turn when the inevitable clash came between his stepson and the rightful king. Elizabeth wondered if more treachery was being plotted.

Life flowed on in the following weeks and she got to know and care for her companions in the castle. John of Lincoln, the son of Richard's sister the Duchess of Suffolk, had been appointed Lieutenant of Ireland, a courtesy title which made him heir to the throne. He had been one of those who had accompanied her when she left London and he brought with him Lord Morley, the husband of one of his sisters, and also John of Gloucester, Richard's bastard son. The latter especially interested Elizabeth. She wondered who the boy's mother had been but dared not ask him outright so she waited for her opportunity to gently probe and so satisfy her curiosity.

It came one cool day when the little company were gathered together in a chamber before a glowing fire of cedar wood, and Elizabeth drew a furred cloak round her with a little shiver. It was John of Gloucester who spoke thoughtfully.

'I wonder if it is as cold in Nottingham where my father resides?'

Elizabeth smiled.

'I expect Uncle Richard has more on his mind than the cold. He is waiting to see when Henry Tudor will move.'

The young man spoke forlornly.

'I would be with my father. Why could I not stay with him?' and he turned to Lincoln, 'You as his heir must remain here in safety but I care not if I lose my life. I would be with him when he goes into battle against the Welsh-man.'

Elizabeth spoke softly. 'Perhaps he cares for you too much to risk your life. You have a sister also who would grieve at your death.'

The answer came quickly.

'Katherine my sister would suffer more if aught befell my father. She, too, loves him as did our mother also.'

The question was asked before Elizabeth realised.

'Who is your mother, John?'

He spoke frankly with no sign of embarrassment.

'She was a great lady who cared for him before he married the Lady Anne. He told me of it so that I would understand. She had loved him when a girl and, after trouble flared between King Edward and Warwick, they met again at Court. She found him truly unhappy, weighed down by the thoughts of Anne Neville and desired to comfort him. Out of that desire I was born and when news came from France that Warwick's daughter had been married to Margaret of Anjou's son he turned more and more to her as time went on until my sister came into the world. But, as you know, the Lady Anne lost her husband and returned to England in great distress, and my father sought for her. His heart was with her and my mother could not hold him. So, as she told me, she relinquished him sadly and returned to her own mother, where she died shortly after being taken with a fever. But he has always cared for us and held our mother in great respect.'

Elizabeth was silent. She could ask no more but her mind was alive with sadness. She looked at the speaker, studying the chestnut hair and deep velvety eyes. So must his mother have looked. For a moment her past feelings for her uncle were re-created and sorrow tore at her until new tidings reached the castle.

Henry Tudor had moved into Wales and was approaching England. With him came his Uncle Jasper, Earl of Pembroke, and those who had fled to Brittany after Buckingham's rebellion, also mercenaries and two thousand men provided by the French King Charles.

The messengers to Sheriff Hutton rode repeatedly to the Yorkshire Castle and the anxious inhabitants heard that on the nineteenth of August the Tudor and King Richard were both riding towards Leicester to face each other. They met on the plain of Redmore, near to the little village of Sutton Cheney, a dozen miles outside the city.

Elizabeth spent two restless nights. In her mind she pictured her uncle waiting for the early morning light and wondered what his thoughts had been as he shared with his men the hopes and fears of the coming day. Did he go back over that life when he was a young boy living in the household of the Earl of Warwick? Of that choice he had been forced to make between his loyalty to Edward on the one hand and his brother George and Warwick on the other? Of his assumption of the crown not by inclination but by necessity and all that followed after. Anxiously she waited for fresh news and on the twenty-second the messenger came and she saw him arrive from a window overlooking the courtyard.

It was John of Gloucester who came to her first, his brown eyes awash with tears, as he held out shaking hands to her.

'My father is dead, killed by the treachery of Lord Stanley, and Henry Tudor is King of England.'

Elizabeth was stunned. Richard no more and that strange man now holding the crown of England.

She spoke constrainedly, grasping the boy's hands.

'John, tell me. I must know all.'

He answered, his voice breaking, 'The men of York did not arrive in time and the King rode to meet the Tudor in single combat. But Stanley gave the word, his troops swept down from the right and beat my father and his faithful few who rode with him into the ground. Lady Bessy, they treated my father like a poltroon, throwing his body unclothed over a miserable nag, the blood welling from his many wounds.'

Now grief gave way to anger and he went on bitterly.

'The Tudor made no move to meet him as one brave man to another. He stood behind his commanders and watched while Stanley did his work for him. God curse him for that day's work.'

Sickened by the terrible tale Elizabeth sought her bedchamber, her thoughts alive with memories of the late King. His kindness to her when she was a child, his love for his wife, his stricken face when she died. The memories came unbidden as she covered her eyes with trembling fingers. But not only did she grieve for a beloved uncle, fears for her own future assailed her. She knew that upon her young body were centred the desires of many people.

The Earl of Richmond now King, his ambitious mother Lady Margaret Beaufort, and also her own mother, saw in her, after the presumed death of her young brothers, the direct line of the house of York. Clearly, they saw that married to the Tudor she could strengthen his claim to be king in the eyes of the English people.

So Elizabeth waited in great trepidation, and a week later Sir Robert Willoughby arrived with orders from the new King Henry the Seventh, who had set out for his capital. She faced the courteous man with his deferential air in the great hall of the castle as he spoke gravely.

'My lady, our gracious king has sent me to conduct you back to his capital.'

The white-faced girl drew herself up proudly as her heart beat fearfully. 'How do I travel, like a prisoner?'

He answered her hastily.

'No, not so. My master has ordered you are to be given into the care of the Queen Dowager, wife of the late King Edward the Fourth whose daughter you are.'

Elizabeth flushed painfully, speaking forthrightly.

'I am also the niece of the late King Richard the Third,' she said and with head held high left the hall.

On her way back to her apartments she saw two figures coming towards her and knew them for John Earl of Lincoln, with his arm round her little cousin Edward, who sobbed miserably under his breath. She spoke, offering him consolation.

'Edward, do not weep. Our uncle is dead and nothing can bring him back.'

It was John of Lincoln who answered her.

'Edward does not weep for Richard, lady, he is very frightened. You are to ride to London in great state but he is to follow at the tail of the procession like a prisoner and he knows not what it means.'

Elizabeth feared she knew what it portended. As the first male heir of the House of York, although his father had been attained, he could be a source of danger to the Tudor, and her fears for the young boy grew.

Everything was now in a state of turmoil. No mention had been made of John of Lincoln's departure or of other members of the household, but the attendants were busy packing Elizabeth's chests and the possessions of the Earl of Warwick, while Sir Robert consulted with the Princess's ladies. A few days later a fine chariot in which she was to ride was brought forward and she bade farewell to her late home.

The journey seemed long and tiring. The weather was close with a great deal of rain and the confines of the vehicle made Elizabeth feel sickly. Also her mental state caused her much uneasiness as she wondered what lay before her.

As she neared London she saw little knots of people gathering in the villages they passed through and fancied she saw pity in their faces. As they entered the gates of the capital the crowds thickened and when they recognised her they waved kerchiefs and caps crying joyfully, 'The Princess Elizabeth, God bless her sweet face.'

All the way to the Palace of Westminster they saluted her, their welcome like balm to her sore heart, but, as she went to join her mother and sisters, the little Earl of Warwick rode on to the Tower and was confined within its walls.

Elizabeth Woodville and her eldest daughter spoke happily together, the older woman's face glowing with triumph.

'You see, my daughter, you may yet ascend the throne as I predicted. Now the King is reunited with his mother, to whom he is much beholden, she will surely persuade him to take you to wife.'

Elizabeth spoke soberly.

'I have heard nothing of any wedding, mother.'

Elizabeth Woodville smiled.

'Give her time, child. Lady Margaret knows how necessary it is to link together the houses of York and Lancaster and will find a means whereby you and your sisters are recognised as legitimate.'

The new King, meanwhile, had been watched by his subjects with mixed emotions. Why, they asked each other, does he ride in a closed chariot like a woman or a prisoner. Not so had they been used to seeing their kings enter the capital, but richly horsed, with destriers tossing their plumed heads and silken banners waving before them.

Henry, however, had no intention of exposing himself to danger from attack by any who still held Richard in love and respect, and meant to be sure that he lived to reign as King. When he reached Shoreditch he saw the Mayor approaching in scarlet robes, together with Aldermen, Councillors and chief citizens and, descending from the coach, he spoke briefly, telling them that he came to claim the throne 'by right of conquest'.

Elizabeth Woodville, hearing of this, stormed and cried to her daughter, fearing that the new conqueror had no intention of implementing the promise made that Christmas Day in Rennes.

The new King kept his own counsel, riding to attend a solemn service in St

Paul's Cathedral, then setting off for the Palace of Sheen, where he took up residence. It was then that a more deadly enemy than any Yorkist began to creep about the streets of London. The sweating sickness manifested itself, raging through the City so that no man thought of anything save his own health and how to safeguard it.

All through the month of September it continued, then, as it began to wane, the Countess of Richmond spoke forcefully to her son.

'Henry, get yourself crowned. There are many doyens of the Yorkist clan who will endeavour to make trouble for you. As King your position will be immeasurably strengthened and you can take action against them.'

Henry agreed, giving orders that the coronation should go ahead even though it could not compare with the pageantry of former kings. He took up residence in the Tower, as was customary, and, on October the thirtieth, rode to the Abbey and was there anointed as the seventh Henry.

The people lined the streets to observe their new monarch, freely criticising every facet of the procession, and Elizabeth and her mother watched from a window. They had not been invited and the mother's heart was torn with doubts.

A few days later the Tudor King made his way to the ladies' chamber in the palace to meet the Queen Dowager and her daughter, the Princess. It was a private meeting and for the first time Elizabeth saw the man who was now her King.

Through the palace corridors he came, accompanied by a figure she recognised, and flanked by men in a costume new to all. They were a personal bodyguard created by the King on the coronation day to guard him against the assassin's weapon. He had named them 'Yeomen of the Guard'.

The face which Elizabeth recognised was that of John Morton, Bishop of Ely.

After being sent by Richard as a prisoner to Brecon he had conspired with Buckingham and, after the failure of the rebellion, had fled abroad to Brittany. Now he was back in England, standing triumphantly as mentor at the side of the younger man.

Elizabeth looked into the face of the new King and he surveyed her with unblinking gaze.

She saw a spare man with fair hair, high cheekboned face, his mouth unsmiling, his eyes steel grey and hard beneath the narrowed lids. He saw a girl of a height comparable with his own, her eyes blue as the summer sky and a face of surpassing loveliness.

His mouth tightened even more and he thought of her father whom he had seen as King. That was in the days when he had lived in the Countess of Pembroke's household before, sensing Edward's hostility, he had fled with his Uncle Jasper to safer ground overseas.

Elizabeth felt dislike of both her mother and herself in his breast as they bent the knee before him and, as he aided them to rise, she shuddered at the touch of his cold, bony hand upon her own.

His voice was formal as he spoke.

'Welcome, madam, you and your daughter have all you desire, I trust?'

Elizabeth Woodville bowed her head in assent, wondering if she dare mention a certain subject lying so close to her heart, but something in the King's manner bade her be wary and she only thanked him formally.

A few minutes later, with an abrupt bow, he was gone, and Elizabeth, her voice shaking, spoke nervously.

'He cannot even speak English properly.'

Her mother turned on her.

'What did you expect? He has always lived on the Continent since a young boy and his speech must ever be marred by it. What should cause you more concern is whether he will take you to wife. Without that we are nothing. Should some old companions of your Uncle Richard try to use you to ferment a rebellion, Henry could have us eliminated as a danger to his throne.'

Elizabeth pondered her mother's words, realising the uncertainty of their position and tried to sustain her hopes for the future.

The people regarded their new King with careful eyes.

Now confirmed in his high office, he repossessed his mother of all her lands and gave to her husband, the Earldom of Derby. A gesture, too, which temporarily raised the hopes of the Dowager followed when he passed an act legitimising Elizabeth and her sisters.

Nothing more happened to nourish their hopes. They lived in luxury surrounded by ladies, pages, and attendants to do their bidding, wearing rich robes and eating from dishes to delight their appetites. Jesters and acrobats wiled away the passing hours, but the little family were forbidden to leave the environs of the palace and suffered no small frustration because of it.

Always over all hung the question asked endlessly by the people. Would he take the Princess as his wife? They wished this wholeheartedly, showing their desire in little outbursts so that the King's spies could hear them.

'He thinks to rule alone. Long ago he promised to marry our Princess. Only then can we be assured of a true King and Queen upon the throne.'

Henry listened. In December the council spoke officially, begging him take as his wife Elizabeth of the true blood of the royal family, and finally he formally consented to do this.

Jubilantly the Queen Dowager received the news and there was great excitement among her younger daughters, but Elizabeth wept quietly to the sister next to her in age.

'I fear him, Cicely, and even more I fear the influence of his mother. He knows it is her plotting which has helped him to attain the throne and I shall have a husband ruled by another woman.'

What she did not disclose to the younger girl was the dread in her heart of the relationship in the marriage-bed. She had known what it was to love another if only in a young girl's innocent way. Her thoughts of her Uncle Richard had meant no more than the longing to be held in his arms and feel his lips on hers.

Now she was confronted with the marital act and she shrank from the thought of it. The touch of that dry hand on hers and the knowledge that he would possess her totally caused feelings of distaste which marred the following days.

January the eighteenth was fixed for the wedding and on that morning she rode through the garlanded streets in an ornate litter with a decorated canopy of silk above it. Her robe was of cloth of silver tissue with a coronet of pearls on her honey-coloured hair, and the latter fell in silken beauty below her waist.

As she passed, the people shouted themselves hoarse, throwing roses of red and white paper into her lap and danced with their arms about one another. In that manner they celebrated the ceremony they so heartily approved.

Standing before the magnificent altar in the Abbey, she felt again his hands on hers and was conscious that a little warmth coursed through its veins. As they turned to leave she felt his gaze on her and raised her eyes to look into his face.

There was a slight smile now on his lips as he spoke quietly.

'It is done, Elizabeth, you are now my wife.'

Grateful for his heartening words she returned his smile timidly and later as she sat beside him at the glittering banquet a measure of comfort stole over her.

The torches were lit in the lofty hall as Margaret Beaufort led her away to where the ladies of the bedchamber waited to disrobe her. Standing in a fur-lined cloak the nineteen-year-old girl heard her new mother-in-law speak softly.

'Elizabeth, remember your duty. The King needs an heir,' and left her standing there alone.

Reluctantly Elizabeth moved towards the luxurious bed and, casting off the heavy robe, climbed mother-naked and shivering into its chilly embrace.

She heard the door open, and the voices of those who accompanied her husband were shrill with lascivious mirth until, with a firm hand he closed it, shutting off their clamour, and came to stand beside her.

He was wearing a velvet robe bordered with marten, his expression inpenetrable, and she shrank back against the pillows, drawing the silken covers up to her throat.

What if she did not bear children to this man, she wondered wildly? How if he was unable to quicken her womb into life? As far as she knew there had been no involvement with women in his troubled life save the daughter of the Earl of Pembroke, and that had been but idle talk. The frightened thoughts coursed through her head until he spoke sombrely, holding out his hand, his eyes fixed on her face.

'Elizabeth, you are not alone in your fears. I, too, must learn to enjoy passion. Will you give yourself to me?'

Her heart steadied, and she bent her head, a wave of sympathy breaking over her at his words. As he divested himself of his robe and joined her in the bed, she put her arms round his thin form.

He needed her understanding as she needed his forbearance and she spoke impulsively.

'Henry, let us comfort each other,' and felt response rise in him.

So Elizabeth the new wife forgot her fears and afterwards slept with her head on her husband's shoulder.

★   ★   ★

In the courtyard of the Palace of Westminster there was great activity.

The grooms of the chamber ran ceaselessly about, supervising the baggage trains which carried all the necessary impedimenta for a royal progress, drinking and eating vessels, mattresses, coverlets, pillows, chamberpots, everything to bring comfort, even cushions to ease the noble bodies when they rested on hard benches.

The great horses of the nobles stood waiting, caparisoned in velvet and tawny damask, the King's charger displaying cloth of gold bordered with fringes of gold thread six inches deep. In the sunlight of the February morning the handsome creatures tossed their heads and pawed the ground as if they knew the King of England was to set off this day to show himself to the common people of his country.

He was to ride as far as York, where the citizens were an unknown factor due to their allegiance to Richard the Third. Since his marriage to their lovely

Princess he had been accepted by the people of London, now he hoped the same welcome would be accorded him as he rode northwards.

Elizabeth stood on the palace steps as he bade her farewell. His lean body was clad in a furred tunic with riding-boots upon his feet, and a short cloak of the royal purple hung from his shoulders.

He held his cap in his hand as he came to salute her and she extended the stirrup-cup which, by tradition, was offered to the monarch on these occasions.

The night before in their private chamber she had told him of a hope that had been born in her breast and he showed himself very conscious of it as he bent to kiss her cheek.

'Elizabeth, take good care of yourself,' he said significantly, then turned to mount his waiting steed.

She sighed to herself. He was a strange man. After the wedding night she had looked for some continuance of the understanding which had been born between them but he had withdrawn into his former shell of indifference, relinquishing it only when he took her in the privacy of their bedchamber.

Now that the first experience was over she had longed to show her husband the new affection which flowed for him in her breast, but, to her dismay, she found no reciprocal feelings in his manner. He used her body as an instrument by which he could bring into the world the heir he so urgently desired and so cement his bargain with his subjects. So she listened to the sound of the great cavalcade grow gradually fainter as it set off for the outskirts of the city, then turned to walk back into the palace.

As his wife it had been her right to attend the King on this occasion, but she knew that his mother had desired to stand there to bid him farewell publicly, save that it would have been commented on by watching eyes. So Lady Margaret had made her leave taking earlier within the palace.

Elizabeth, in the month since the wedding, had come to realise that certain fears she had entertained were being proved beyond all doubt. Margaret Beaufort, she saw, was the force behind her son, and Elizabeth was conscious of disillusionment as to her position. Even now she was not Queen, only the wife of the King, and resentment stirred sometimes in her breast.

Her mother-in-law had been married twice, first to Edmund Tudor, Duke of Richmond, and later to Lord Stanley, now Earl of Derby. She was a wealthy woman as well as a clever one and when her son Henry seized the crown at Bosworth she began to take a great interest in what was called the New Learning. But why, Elizabeth asked herself, should she a Princess by birth come only second in control of the Court to Margaret Beaufort. True, the lady was a direct descendant of John of Gaunt and her father had been the Earl of Somerset, but that gave her no right to assume the role which should of right belong to Henry's wife. The New Learning believed that women had a duty to guide and assist men in a world whose rule until now had been their sole perogative. The lady's endowment of two colleges at Cambridge, those of Christ's and St John's, and the taking over of Caxton's printing presses, which had been so lavishly aided by both her father and Uncle Richard, were all very praiseworthy but the Countess carried them to excess.

So thought Elizabeth as she made her way towards the solar and found her mother-in-law already there sitting with a book of the household accounts upon her knee. She wore the robes of an abbess, having taken a vow of chastity in which she refused to cohabit with her husband but relinquished not one iota of her power at Court, remaining a powerful woman rather than a religious recluse.

She looked up as Elizabeth entered, nodding briefly, then returned to her perusal of its contents. Searching for understanding between them Elizabeth spoke gently, 'Lady mother, I have news for you.'

Margaret's eyes fixed themselves upon her daughter-in-law, her eyes sharp. 'Indeed, Bessy, tell me.'

Elizabeth's voice faltered as she met the piercing gaze.

'I have passed my month end and feel I must be with child.'

A look of triumph stole over the older woman's features and she closed the book, 'The King should have been told of this before he left,' she said.

Elizabeth laughed.

'But of course he knows. Naturally, he would be the first to whom I would speak of it.'

Margaret looked at her disapprovingly, her mouth drawn down at the corners. 'Surely the King's mother is better able to judge when the Sovereign with his many duties should be informed.'

Elizabeth clasped her hands tightly

together, speaking sharply, 'As his wife I do not agree. Between myself and my husband should surely be private understanding.'

Margaret Beaufort reddened angrily and her tone was cold as she spoke. 'Remember, Elizabeth, you are not yet crowned Queen. I see no reason why his mother should not be the first to hear such tidings, so pertinent to the well-being of the crown.'

Her daughter-in-law turned away, conscious of anger rising in her breast which horrified her by its very intensity. Also besides anger was trepidation. Lady Margaret had spoken truly. She was not yet crowned and had no official position within this Tudor court.

So she said nothing more of it through the following weeks, while news came of the King's progress. He paused at Lincoln for the Easter celebrations, then moved on to Nottingham, Pomfret, and so to York. Of these journeys the Court was kept always informed until from York came grave news.

It was Lady Margaret, as she was now known about the Court, who spoke of it to Elizabeth, her eyes burning with anger.

'There has been insurrection in the city of York. It was always loyal to Richard and now his friends Francis Lovell together with Humphrey and Thomas Stafford have taken arms against the King.'

They learned later that Jasper Tudor, Henry's uncle, had ridden to aid him and the rebels were overcome. Humphrey Stafford was brought back to London and hanged, but Thomas, being proved to be but a tool in his brother's hands, was pardoned.

Hearing this Lady Margaret spoke bitterly to Elizabeth.

'Who do you think has given shelter to Lovell? None other than the usurper's sister, Margaret of Burgundy.'

Elizabeth flinched. It was her mother-in-law's name for Richard, which she always used, making the younger woman's nerves quiver. Why did she always stress it, thought the girl, knowing that he was her uncle and his niece might have affection for him.

But Lady Margaret had no compunction about driving into the young wife that the Plantagenets were a tainted race and the newly-risen house of Tudor the saviours of England.

After York, all went forward as Henry desired and the people of England, thankful that at last a King and his wife sat on the throne, gave him an approving welcome.

One day Elizabeth was shown in no uncertain terms exactly what her position was. It was Lady Margaret who had a document brought to her and whose gimlet eyes watched her face as she read. It was a copy of the Pope's Bull of Confirmation regarding the marriage, stating that after the joining together of King Henry of the house of Lancaster and the Princess Elizabeth of the house of York, his Holiness approved that the offspring of their bodies should be heirs to the throne of England.

As she came to the last part of the document Elizabeth felt the hot colour rise in her face. It stated that should the said Elizabeth decease without issue between them, any future child born between the King and another wife should be made inheritor of that same realm of England.

She had known this from the first, but seeing it set out there in the document while his babe lay beneath her heart caused terrible frustration to assail her. Surely if she died in childbirth, then would be the time, when he took another wife, to request a fresh statement from his Holiness.

Her hands trembled as she handed back the parchment and without comment retired. Once in her own chamber she could give way to her outraged feelings in disillusioned tears.

In August the King returned to his capital to be welcomed by the family.

Elizabeth saw how his eyes wandered over her developing figure as he saluted her, then turned triumphantly to Lady Margaret standing beside him.

'I return to happy news,' he said and smiled. She heard her own mother's sardonic laugh as she spoke to sister Cicely.

'Surely it is my daughter who carries his babe,' she said significantly.

Only by the tightening of her lips did Elizabeth know that Lady Margaret had heard the words, for she made no comment and appeared otherwise unaware of them.

Later Elizabeth Woodville spoke scornfully to her daughter. 'You give too much credence to the Lady's position. I hear that plans for the lying-in ceremony and everything connected with the birth are under her control. My daughter, you must give voice to your desires. You are the mother-to-be.'

Elizabeth agreed with her and one day sought Lady Margaret's company, speaking boldly to her,

'Lady mother, I would have some say in the ordering of my chamber. I desire also to choose the decorating of the cradle and decide by whom my babe should be nursed.'

Calmly as one speaking to a child the Lady answered her,

'My daughter, you are but twenty years of age and for the first time a mother. I am at the King's express wish taking all these affairs out of your hands.'

Elizabeth spoke hotly.

'I am sure Henry would allow me to have my way in this matter.'

The answer came coldly.

'Do you think I speak untruly, Elizabeth. It would cause much anger in the King's breast if you thought that.'

Elizabeth caught her breath. She was too uncertain of Henry's support of her to speak again and, feeling great heartache, she desisted.

So Lady Margaret, mother of the King, controlled the court and all thought that only through her could the ear of the Sovereign be reached. But great as was her influence Henry had a mind of his own and only when he had listened to his mother's exhortations did he decide for himself the best course to pursue.

As the weeks passed, however, it seemed that Lady Margaret abated much her stern manner, speaking in charitable tones to the pregnant girl, until at the eighth month Elizabeth retired into the specially appointed chamber in the castle at Winchester.

The birth was due on October the eighteenth, according to the physicians, but it was customary to retire for at least a month before the date in case they were at fault in their calculations and also to save the mother-to-be embarrassment at this time.

So Elizabeth bade farewell to the outside world, taking up residence in apartments from which all light was excluded save that from one small window. The flames of the cedar wood fires illuminated the scene around which moved Elizabeth Woodville and the Lady Margaret, together with other ladies to act as attendants during the time of waiting.

To her surprise Elizabeth found that her mother-in-law had arranged all with her own tastes in mind.

She had been pleasurably enough consulted as to her choice of chamber furnishings and was delighted to find they had been carried out, the tapestries showing birds and flowers in delicate colours while sumptuous carpets overlaid the floors. The great bed which stood ready to receive so great a prince or princess was rich in coverings of velvet and fur with entwined roses of red and white silk embroidered on pillows and bed hangings.

Her chapel, too, was beautiful, the gold plate sparkling with precious stones, the crucifixes of ivory lying on the altar, while with them lay the holy relics to give aid and comfort during the birth.

At first there was an air of tension in the rooms, but conscious of the Queen's feelings and the need for harmony, the two mothers sought to disguise their enmity and control their tongues.

One in whose company Elizabeth found great pleasure was Margaret Plantagenet, the daughter of George of Clarence and Isabel Neville. She was the sister of that young Edward with whom Elizabeth had lived at Sheriff Hutton and when Elizabeth had married she had asked that the grave, sweet-natured girl might be included in her household.

So during the time of waiting they talked together and their conversation often centred upon this boy, while the King's wife cheered Margaret with happy memories of the Yorkshire Castle, reassuring her too that he was well cared for in the Tower. Another topic which took Elizabeth's mind off the approaching birth was touched on one day.

Sir Richard Pole, her Chamberlain, was a man with a fine face and upright bearing, a cousin of Henry Tudor's, for his mother and Lady Margaret were sisters. It was he who had ushered Elizabeth into her prepared chamber for the confinement with sincere wishes for 'a good hour' and Margaret Plantagenet mentioned him as they sat together.

'Sir Richard Pole gave lustre to your withdrawal time, Your Grace.'

Elizabeth felt a smile touch her lips at the artless comment.

'Indeed, Margaret, he is a fine man and one in which any woman might find a good husband.'

The young girl's eyes shone as she replied,

'Indeed a wife might learn much from such a man.'

Striving not to show her amusement Elizabeth spoke with due soberness, 'I am sure he would be a tender teacher. How feel you about him?'

Margaret dropped her embroidery

needle into her lap, forgetting propriety as she clasped her hands together.

'Oh, Your Grace, I would be very happy to be tutored by him.'

The Queen had seen the looks that the man of thirty had cast upon the young girl and wondered if such a match would ever take place, but three days later, to her astonishment, she realised that at eight months the babe was on its way.

Swiftly those around her were alerted and she began the process of bringing forth her first child. Lifted on to the birth pallet she was conscious of the many figures around her and of one in particular whose hand grasped hers as the pains grew in intensity.

Between the agonising bouts she looked up into the face above hers.

'Lady mother,' she moaned.

The response came back immediately, 'Be brave, my daughter. You bear a royal child,' and the Countess of Richmond's voice encouraged and sustained her.

It was some hours later that the same voice spoke triumphantly, affection lighting its owner's face.

'You have a son, Elizabeth,' and the healthy, squalling infant was laid in her arms. She looked down at the wrinkled face reddened by its own clamour and her heart was thankful. Her husband had his heir and this small mortal would now one day, God willing, be King of this England of hers.

Elizabeth slept and woke to find her husband standing by her. Tenderness showed in his eyes as he stooped to kiss first her brow and then her hand.

'Thank you, Elizabeth, now you must be crowned,' and Lady Margaret smiled, touching her shoulder gently.

★   ★   ★

The baptism in Winchester Cathedral was a lavish affair with all the nobles of the court attending, walking in procession to the font of silver gilt in which a fine linen cloth had been laid to receive

218

the precious little form. Only one figure was missing: the Earl of Oxford, godfather to the Prince, had not arrived, as being still on his estates in the West he had been caught by the child's sudden arrival in the world.

The service was in full voice as Cicely, carrying the child in its priceless robes, walked to the font and he was given the name of Arthur. Henry had decided this, providing it was a son, before the birth, in the hope that he would follow in the footsteps of the legendary figure from whom he himself claimed descent.

His grandmother Elizabeth Woodville had just laid him on the altar when Oxford arrived, but he was in time to receive him for the confirmation and to hear the trumpets ring out their crystal sounds.

As they returned to the palace, the members of the family gathered round to give their gifts, gold cups, silver gilt spoons the handles of which were inlaid with precious stones, a coffer of gold pieces and many more.

Joyfully the King and Queen received the congratulations of the Dowager Queen, the baby's Aunts Cicely, Anne, Margaret and Bridget while beside them stood watchfully the other royal grandmother.

The courtiers noted how she gave her orders and the infant was carried away at her bidding but Elizabeth ignored it, conscious of the care she had received in her time of need and willing herself to encourage a better relationship with the Countess.

It was at this time that Elizabeth began to illustrate a beautiful missal, into which she copied the likenesses of her favourite saints, decorating it with white roses, the emblem of the house of York.

This gave her many hours of pleasure until intrigue cast a shadow across the Court.

It was the King who first spoke of it to her. Henry had asked her to accompany him to the royal nursery where their little son lived, tended by two nurses, a third to suckle the child, physicians to care for his health, and the squires of his body to be always watchful about him.

Having satisfied themselves that all was well they returned to their own chambers, where the King viewed his wife uneasily.

'Bessy,' and he used the familiar name which he so seldom did, 'there is a rumour going about which my spies are probing that the Earl of Lincoln, who has fled from Sheriff Hutton, has joined Francis Lovell in Burgundy. They are now in touch with some dissident priest who puts forward an illegal claim. He says that a pupil of his, a boy called Lambert Simnel, is the Earl of Warwick newly escaped from the Tower. As you know, Edward is secure in the fortress but as my wife you must give me all your support to kill this rumour in the eyes of the people.'

He took steps then to bring the little Earl from the Tower and, showing herself with her ladies, Elizabeth stood on a balcony watching the boy she remembered, paraded through the streets to give lie to the tale. Beside her stood one sobbing bitterly and Elizabeth spoke gently to her.

'Margaret, your little brother is alive and well. See how he rides jauntily in rich garments on a fine steed.'

The girl shook her head.

'Nay, Your Grace. I see a young boy with vacant eyes and a smile as if he knows not what goes on around him. Edward was always a tender plant as Aunt Anne once told me, he should be treated with loving care. Now incarceration has dulled his senses and he is but a shadow of the brother I knew.'

But the people of England who saw him pass knew that the Earl of Warwick was still held by King Henry and, when the pretender's supporters met outside Newark a great number had defected because of the King's action.

At Stoke-on-Trent on June the Fourteenth Henry's army under the

Earl of Oxford met Simnel's forces of eight thousand men under his experienced captain, Martin Swartz, but there were Irishmen and foreign auxiliaries who were untrained fighters in his army and the troops of the Earl soon gained ascendancy.

Amongst those who perished were the Earl of Lincoln, who had been King Richard's heir but who had made no move to gain the crown for himself, Sir Thomas Broughton, Knight of the Garter, Thomas and Maurice Fitzgerald, and the captain himself Martin Swartz, while Francis Lovell fled and was never seen again.

Henry with the eyes of the Continent upon him, to show his contempt, put Simnel as a scullion in his kitchens but later he was allowed to tend the King's birds and became eventually head falconer.

During this time Elizabeth, knowing her husband's innocence in this matter, rode on every occasion possible to give him support so that the people, who loved her dearly, sided with the King and cheered him lustily whenever he rode abroad.

One evening, as they rose from the board and settled themselves to watch a masque performed by members of the Court, Henry spoke gratefully to her.

'I thank you, Elizabeth, for your upholding of me during these past weeks. A wife such as you deserves the support of her husband,' and she wondered if he had in mind her crowning. He was indeed a man difficult to understand, this Tudor King. His hands were careful upon the pursestrings of his treasury but unexpectedly lavish where diplomacy was needed to impress ambassadors and visitors to his country.

To Elizabeth, used to the extravagance of her father's Court and the open-handedness of her Uncle Richard, her husband's nature seemed at times miserly.

It was heightened by his chief

councillor and the guardian of his purse.

Bishop Morton, soon raised to the Archbishopric of Canterbury, was also his Chancellor, and this man instituted a system which was to bring a great deal of gold into Henry's coffers.

He spoke of it one day to the King, a crafty smile playing about his lips.

'Your Grace, I have had serious thoughts concerning your position as King. Is it not true that no abundance of gold can be too much for the Sovereign who has an army to maintain, also that every man and his possessions belong to that Sovereign? I consider now a new law by which your people can be encouraged to assist you.

'Should any man be found to spend much, he should release a portion of what is left to you. Also those who spend little can turn over a goodly portion of their savings to reimburse you in the running of the country.'

Henry looked at his Chancellor and inwardly marvelled at the duplicity of the man. Here was one whose thoughts ran parallel with his own and a faithful servant to boot. But he carefully concealed his jubilation, merely nodding thoughtfully in acquiescence.

'It is a good ruling,' he said crisply.

So the device to extract money from the wealthy merchants and all who held positions of repute came into being and caused much resentment against the two councillors, Richard Empson and Edmund Dudley, who carried it out. Only the people gave it the name of 'Morton's Fork' after the new implement being always more widely used at the tables of the prosperous.

One day the wife of the King received tidings which caused her great sorrow and bewilderment, straining the new kinder relationship between herself and the Countess of Richmond. Her sister Cicely came to speak to her with trembling lips and reddened eyelids,

'Bessy, prepare yourself for sad news. Our mother has been sent from Court and forced to move to Bermondsey

Abbey, which she always supported during her days as Queen. The King has confiscated all her possessions, giving her only a small pension to live in quiet retirement.'

Elizabeth stared at her sister's frightened face.

'I cannot believe it. She stood as godmother to our son. Surely some terrible mistake has been made. I must see the King immediately.'

But the King was closeted with his councillors all that day and through the evening and it was night when her ladies had disrobed and left her that she waited for him to visit her. As the door of the chamber opened she sat upright in the bed, her hair tumbling about her shoulders and burst into angry speech.

'Henry, what is this I hear. My mother has been sent from Court with no reason given.'

He avoided her gaze, turning to discard the robe he wore.

'She is a mischievous woman giving expression to thoughts not worthy of the grandmother of the heir to the throne.'

Elizabeth felt the rebellious tears rise in her eyes as she spoke unwisely.

'Although you will not admit it, I know the reason. Your mother thinks she should rule the Court while I am of little account. My mother does not agree with her, that is why she must be shut away. Shame on you.'

'Silence, Elizabeth. I owe my life and my crown to my mother's devotion. Without her I would not now be King.'

His eyes were cold as he met her gaze and his wife drew a deep breath, biting back the reckless words now forming. Like a spider, Lady Margaret had spun her web of intrigue in King Richard's reign on her son's behalf and only through that King's clemency had she been spared imprisonment. But it would not be wise to remind Henry of these facts and she clutched at the pillows beneath her in frustration.

Henry's hand fell on her arm.

'You must not question my actions

nor those of my mother,' he said. The anger had died out of his voice as he put a hand under her chin and tilted her face towards him.

'You are my wife,' he said and his eyes scrutinised her closely, noting the beauty of the face so close to his own.

His thin mouth came down on hers in demanding appetite and his arms closed round her as he joined her in the bed. She suffered him silently but her thoughts were bitter as the passion rose in him, and as he panted and struggled over her body she rejected him in her heart . . .

Later he surveyed her gloomily, conscious of her resentment.

'Learn your position, Elizabeth,' he said and returned to his own chamber.

For some time after that night the better relationship between the King and his wife weakened until one day Lady Margaret spoke privately to the Sovereign.

'Henry, you have a child but the boy's mother is not yet Queen. Is it not time you rectified the matter?' Elizabeth found then, to her surprise, that he had given orders for the coronation to take place and her sore heart knew some surcease.

The news was soon spread about and the thoughts of the people turned towards the great entertainment the coronation of Elizabeth of York and the final accolade in her position in English eyes.

On November the twenty-fifth the people gathered in their warmest clothes, talking excitedly in high good-humour.

The King had seen the wisdom of what they had so forcibly shown to be their will and now that beloved Princess was to share the throne in her own right.

The highways were gaily decorated, with tapestries hanging from every window, while coloured streamers were knotted round pillars and doorways. The streets were freshly strewn with sand on which both horses and men on foot might walk in safety, while, above, the pale November sun cast its beneficial rays upon the scene.

The centre of all these preparations found it difficult to believe that it was really happening and as she was prepared for the ceremony her heart beat high with excitement mixed with fear. She could hear the hum of voices like a swarm of bees rising faintly from without the palace walls and stood with trembling limbs as her ladies robed her.

First, they put on her a gown of velvet, the rich folds falling round her feet, then draped a mantle of the royal purple edged with ermine about her shoulders. Then came the Lady Margaret to set a circlet of gold upon her silken hair, and she spoke to the excited girl under her breath.

'Be calm and controlled, my daughter.'

With her sister Cicely holding her train, Elizabeth walked out through the gateway of the Tower to enter the litter draped in cloth of gold waiting for her, and acknowledged the waving hands of the common people who vociferously acclaimed her day.

Outside the doors of Westminster Hall she descended and took her place in the waiting procession. It was formed of knights, heralds, and the nobles of the kingdom dressed in their magnificent robes of purple, scarlet, blue and that new colour 'goose turd green'. The notable prelates of the Church, mitred bishops and abbots stood ready to walk behind the members of the Abbey's hierarchy holding aloft crucifixes and satin banners depicting the lives of the saints.

Elizabeth took her own position behind Jasper, Duke of Bedford, the King's uncle, who carried the sparkling crown on a purple velvet cushion with the Duke of Suffolk preceding him, bearing the jewelled sceptre and orb.

On her right the Bishop of Ely supported her and, seeing how pale she grew with emotion, spoke in encouraging tones. So with the Duchesses following in their satin gowns, holding their coronets, she walked the short distance to the holy edifice, the clamour of the Abbey bells sounding in her ears.

As she paused in the doorway she heard the cries of rejoicing behind her change to the ugly sounds of fear as the screams of frightened people vied with shouted commands to assault her ears.

She turned her head to see the procession behind her cast into confusion, her ladies clutching their coronets to their breasts as they cowered against the stone pillars while the officers of the court tried to restrain the milling crowd. A voice spoke in Elizabeth's ear,

'Fear not, Your Grace. It is but some of the people who try as is customary to gain possession of a piece of the coronation carpet you have walked over. In their eagerness to gain so coveted an object they have cut it up with knives and disrupted the procession.'

The owner of the voice departed and, shaken, Elizabeth resumed her progress.

In the tranquillity of the Abbey the strident bells became muted as the doors were closed and the saints and angels stared down at her from the stained glass windows while the voices of the choristers chanted softly.

Slowly Elizabeth made her way to where the throne with its golden cushions waited and took her seat upon it. Before the altar with its flickering candles stood the Bishop of Winchester to anoint her on forehead and breast and to bless the coronation ring which he placed on her finger. Finally, the symbol of her position, the crown, rested upon her head and the sceptre and orb were handed to her.

Now the voices of the choir burst forth in adoration, the sound rising to the vaulted roof as the Duchesses placed their coronets upon their heads and the Mass was celebrated.

Light pouring through the great stained glass window glowed with unearthly beauty as it fell on the rich altar, turning its treasury of chalices, plates, and cups, together with the robes of the officiating priests, into a kaleidoscope of colour.

As the Queen moved to the shrine of St Edward and placed her crown momentarily upon the small altar there, she raised her eyes to where on a platform fronted by a wooden screen sat her husband and his mother. Custom forbade that the King should take part in the ceremony but he could watch with satisfaction, knowing that it was through his decree that the ritual had taken place.

The ending of the ceremony brought Elizabeth now crowned to a private chamber where she knew a short respite before the traditional banquet.

It was Margaret Plantagenet who answered her anxious enquiries soothingly, 'It meant little, Your Grace. Some of the crowd, anxious lest they should not receive their piece of the carpet jostled us, but we soon recovered.'

At her word one of the younger Duchesses burst into tears,

'It was fearsome. They fought like wild beasts and we believed they might turn their anger upon us.'

Margaret spoke tersely.

'Stop your wailing, you trouble the Queen. It was but love for her which made them act so.' One of the older women laughed shortly.

'Rather it was greed to own something of great value. The Sergeant-at-Arms gave his orders and many were taken into custody. By this time they will have paid a heavy penalty for their misdoings.'

In the following days the Queen felt immense comfort in her assured position and also the company of her baby son. Born as he was to a great destiny his mother decided that as he grew older she would try to implant in his young mind the characteristics which she held so dear. Respect for the King his father, affection for the royal grandmother, and for herself the knowledge of her love and that he could always turn to her in joy or sorrow.

He was barely two years old when the King, coming to join her one day in the nursery, contemplated the child as he took his early steps.

'The boy grows rapidly. This day will mean much to him in the future, Bessy.'

'Why this day especially, my husband,' she asked.

He started to pace about the apartment, watched by those in charge of the infant who had retired out of earshot when the King entered.

'I have come straight from the council chamber to tell you important news. Today I received from the Spanish Ambassadors a message sent by Ferdinand and Isabella. They accept my proposal that their new daughter Caterina should be affianced to our son. It is a great diplomatic gesture and a truly magnificent uniting of England and Spain.'

Elizabeth felt the facile tears fill her eyes as she said regretfully,

'He is such a baby, barely two years old.'

The King shook his head.

'I have no patience with such ideas,' he said testily, 'our son's future bride is of the purest blood and you should be joyful at the news.'

Elizabeth blinked away the drops he found so unworthy, attempting to justify them.

'Perhaps it is my condition which causes these feelings' she faltered. 'Henry, I think I am with child again.'

With a rare gesture for so undemonstrative a man he threw his velvet cap into the air and came to clasp her hands, 'What better news to excuse your reasoning,' he said heartily and she knew she was forgiven for her unbecoming thoughts.

In 1489 the King and Queen knew great pleasure in the birth of a little daughter named Margaret after the King's mother. The Countess had relaxed even more her domineering ways towards her daughter-in-law and gradually Elizabeth began to feel that her rightful position was being accorded her and that her life was settling down into the calm ways of motherhood.

When her little son was three years of age his father had created him Prince of Wales, and in 1490 a second daughter was born.

Henry came to her as she lay in warm comfort after the birth, 'She must be given your name, my wife. If she grows into the woman her mother is, she will give joy to us all.'

Never before had he spoken so openly to her of his feelings, and Elizabeth felt her heart leap with pleasure.

'Thank you, Henry,' she said softly and as if embarrassed by his own words he patted her hand awkwardly.

Elizabeth saw now that she rode high in her husband's regard. Around her she was gathering an atmosphere which soothed and delighted all, and in 1491 there arrived another son. Seeing his family grow, Henry gave his own name to the handsome boy and contemplated his little brood with growing delight while his beautiful wife drew ever closer to him.

Always the King spent long hours in the council chamber but in his moments of relaxation he joined the Queen to listen to the chatter of the little Prince of Wales, the struggles of the little girls to emulate their elder brother and the resounding cries of the baby Henry.

Later when the children had been removed, the King played cards or chess with the Queen and her ladies, listened to the witty jests of the Queen's personal dwarf Patch and enjoyed the playing of the lute or other stringed instrument, plucked by some chosen musician from the minstrels attached to the royal household.

The boy Henry had just celebrated his first birthday when sadness touched Elizabeth again with its chilly fingers.

She was sitting one evening in her solar with her children about her. Arthur, now six years of age, was shortly to leave London to hold his own court in far away Ludlow, Margaret at three was already showing signs of that wilfulness which was to be such a facet of her nature all her life, and the little Elizabeth, now two years of age, was a happy, lovable child adored by all who knew her. The baby Henry still spent much time in the nursery but was thriving well, and as she waited for her husband she thought how tranquillity now surrounded her.

The understanding between herself and the King developed daily and she treasured this. Now a mature woman, she could think of her love for Uncle Richard as a tender memory and turn towards the father of her children.

She had begun to see that the insecurity which had overshadowed him when he came to the throne had been heightened by the Lambert Simnel uprising and he had clung, although unconsciously, to the only being he completely trusted — his mother.

Only since the coronation, and the more stable relationship between the two women, had his feeling for her changed and, responding to this, she herself had turned more willingly to him. Physical passion was now heightened by affection and as she waited for him she surveyed the fruits of their association with a contented eye.

As the King entered she extended her hand in welcome and he seated himself beside her, his eyes searching her face. 'Bessy, I have news which will cause you much sorrow. For the children's sake try not to be overwhelmed by it.'

With sinking heart she met his gaze. 'It is my mother.'

He bowed his head.

'How did you know?'

She could not answer that question. Only some instinct had warned her, for, visiting the Dowager Queen at regular intervals, she had seen how the weight of years showed more unkindly on the once beautiful face and the scheming characteristics became reduced to the ashes of former passions.

The King went on.

'The messenger has ridden from Bermondsey to say she is failing and I have given orders that your sisters should set off immediately. In your condition I feel it would not be wise to take even so small a journey but should you desire it I will have arrangements made.'

He paused, waiting for her reaction and she felt the sobs rise in her throat. The movement of the new child controlled her and she spoke brokenly,

'I dare not travel, for the sake of the babe. My prayers and thoughts must be with my mother at this time.'

So Elizabeth Woodville ended her long and troubled life in the presence of her four daughters and the Queen's sorrow was heightened by the death of the baby boy born later that year.

* * *

Now the storm clouds of trouble began to gather again, blown across the seas from Margaret of Burgundy's kingdom.

A merchant vessel from Lisbon had entered the harbour of Cork in Ireland amongst its passengers a certain Peter Warbeck. As he walked about the streets of the tiny town the people's interest was drawn to this tall stranger with the charming mien and handsome face.

They talked among themselves.

'He is a fine lad,' they agreed, 'more like a prince than any of us.'

From amongst them a voice spoke out.

'He is like the English King Edward. I saw him once when I visited that country. The boy resembles him.'

Another spoke reprovingly,

'More like his son,' and a third chimed in,

'Yes, a son grown to manhood.'

Excitement grew, invading the little town, and finally as if reluctant the young man revealed his identity.

'Yes,' he told them. 'I am the younger of the two little Princes. I am Richard Plantagenet. My brother was foully murdered in the Tower but I escaped. Now I will try to regain my heritage.'

He did not long remain in Ireland, but, gathering a small crowd of adherents about him, travelled first to France then on to Flanders with high hopes in his heart.

Margaret of Burgundy, the Dowager Duchess, living retired in her own lands, heard of his arrival. She had known great sorrow mixed with intense anger when Henry Tudor had taken the crown at Bosworth and treated her brother's body in such a callous and heartless manner. Although having little power now in Burgundy she watched events in other countries with interest and, when Warbeck arrived in Flanders, the great question occupied her mind. Was he, as he claimed, indeed her nephew, the son of Edward King of England? She waited but the Duke of Burgundy made no move and so she herself sent for the young man, agreeing to see him at her own court.

In the hall of audience she sat in a

high, carved chair, her hands resting tightly on the arms and watched as the slim figure advanced towards her, then as he made obeisance she drew in her breath sharply. Although she had seen little of her two nephews who had been born after her departure to be married, she had met them when she returned to England in 1480. They were boys of ten and eight at that time and this was a man who stood before her — and what a man.

She stared at the youth facing her and saw again the lineaments of her late brother and, rising to her feet, she looked down at the golden head bent before her. She extended her hand and he put his lips to it.

'Aunt Margaret,' he said and his voice was filled with affection. She felt her eyes fill with tears.

'Richard, welcome to Burgundy,' she said and sealed her belief in him with the words.

So Peter Warbeck took up his residence at Margaret's court and she accepted him as the nephew he purported to be, keeping him beside her for many months.

Many Yorkists residing in her lands championed his cause, including secretly some members of the English King's court, and, becoming aware of this, Henry sent two of his spies, Sir Robert Clifford and William Barley, to seek out the truth of the matter. They returned with shattering news. Warbeck was gaining adherents as he travelled and had written to Isabella of Spain and the King of France, asking for aid in his cause.

Towards the end of that year several men holding high positions at Henry's court were arrested and amongst those named were Lord Fitzwalter, Sir Simon Montford, Sir Thomas Thwaites and, most alarming of all, Sir William Stanley.

This man was the brother-in-law of Lady Margaret, mother of the King. Her husband, the Earl of Derby, had been Lord Stanley at the time of

Bosworth and Sir William had joined him in destroying Richard in that battle. Now a rich and powerful knight of Henry's court and chamberlain to the King, he was reputed to have said that 'if he were sure Warbeck was Edward's son he would never fight against him.'

When Elizabeth heard of his arrest she sought the Countess in her own apartments and found a troubled woman who rose to meet her. She met the Queen's gaze with erect form and steady eye.

'My husband and I know nothing of this,' she said proudly. 'We cannot understand how Sir William could behave so. Always my son has rewarded him for his partisanship of the house of Tudor and we have sustained a bitter shock. My husband is devastated by the news.'

Her voice trembled as she spoke and Elizabeth moved to comfort her.

'The King holds no bad opinion of you in this matter. As for me, I am certain that this boy is not my young brother.'

Shortly afterwards the arrested men were brought to trial and all found guilty. They suffered death upon Tower Hill, but Henry paid privately for Sir William's burial at Sion, while Lady Margaret and her husband retired to Latham Hall to recover from their shame and sorrow.

Elizabeth pondered this affair which involved her sisterly affections so closely. She remembered the letter King Richard had written to her mother in which he had stated that at his request the late Duke of Buckingham had taken the two little princes and housed them at Breconbridge. This did not tally with Warbeck's account of the murder of the elder child and the young one's escape from the Tower and, believing her Uncle's version of the tale, she knew that Warbeck must be another imposter.

For several months Perkin, as he was sometimes called, remained at Margaret of Burgundy's court but she saw how, as time went on, his manner became restless, and in the middle of July 1495 she provided him with a number of troops and he set out for Deal. But the English people repulsed him fiercely, capturing one hundred and seventy of his men whom Henry hanged, and their leader returned to Margaret, chastened and anxious.

But now in 1496 Philip of Burgundy concluded a treaty with Henry in which it was arranged that any enemy of either sovereign should be driven out of their respective countries, and the Duke brought pressure to bear upon Margaret so that, reluctantly, she bade farewell to her protégé. He crossed the sea to Scotland, and James the Fourth, the Scottish King, welcomed him. He had no love for the English and their Sovereign and he showed himself willing to consider the claim of the young man to the crown of that country. So he found him apartments in the Castle of Stirling and one day sent for him in private audience.

Stirling was built upon a massive rock and the room in which James received him seemed chill as the winds whined without, but a great fire blazed upon the hearth and beside the King stood a slim dark-haired girl.

James received him cordially.

'I have investigated your claim to be the son of Edward, late King of England, and noted your letters to Isabella of Spain and the King of France. I have examined, too, your letter to a certain Sir Bernard de Fosse, who in his time was the envoy of both your reputed father and Richard the Third, asking him to favour your cause. You sign it 'Your friend Richard of England' and I find it remarkable for its English character. Since you have been here I have deliberately drawn you into contact with two of my most cultured noblemen, Gavin Douglas and William Dunbar, and they speak highly of your abilities. Therefore I am willing to advance your cause and lend you men to achieve it.'

Warbeck's spirits lightened and he turned his eyes on the lady beside the King.

'This is my kinswoman, the Lady Katherine Gordon, sister of the Earl of Huntly. To show my belief in your mission I will give her to you in marriage and provide you with an army.'

The beautiful woman met his gaze with a shy smile and he bent over her hand, conscious of a feeling of disbelief at this change in his fortunes, but he grew to realise that this was no dream when a few days later he stood in the castle chapel. There he and Katherine Gordon were made man and wife and he and she were allotted rooms in the palace suitable for partners in marriage.

That night, as they retired to a great bedchamber, Perkin looked at his bride, speaking hesitantly,

'Katherine, the King has given you to me but I have no way of knowing your own feelings. Forgive me if it causes you sorrow. We have had little chance to get to know each other.'

The colour came and went as she smiled, her hands extended towards him.

'I am not unhappy. As a ward of the King's I always knew I must wed any man he chose for me. My husband, believe me I feel nothing but pleasure that he should choose one so personable to me.'

He put his arms round her then and willingly she went into his embrace. Lifting her in strong arms he carried her to the massive bed and set himself to win her confidence. She responded eagerly and later she sighed softly,

'Oh, my husband, the King could not have given me one for whom I feel greater love.'

So their marriage was consummated with great satisfaction and Peter Warbeck rejoiced in the beauty and amiability of his bride.

Buttressed by a Scottish army numbering fourteen hundred men he entered the northern part of England only to suffer defeat, returning discomforted to Scotland. Henry, meanwhile, had demanded and received a large grant from Parliament for the defence of the realm and his army stood ready to repel any attack.

The Queen of England took small note of these events. She was wrapped in her own private sorrow. Her little daughter Elizabeth had been taken ill and the beloved child died suddenly, leaving a sad gap in her mother's life. To the King, absorbed in the great issues involving his kingdom, the sorrow was not so acute and his wife suffered much of this tragedy alone.

One day, however, he came to her, taking her hands as she sat in sad remembrance.

'Bessy, war is declared against Scotland and we must prepare for Warbeck setting foot again on England's soil. I am sending you and the children to the Tower for safety.'

Elizabeth gave a little cry,

'There is no need, surely, my husband. We can meet this threat together.'

He smiled at her.

'You are my wife. I shall feel happier to know you and our family are safe behind its walls. Do not fear! James will soon realise how few of my people will welcome this Perkin and what a small number he commands to stand against the power of England.'

So Elizabeth with a distressed heart retired with Princess Margaret and Prince Henry into the palace of the Tower and once again she knew the throne was in jeopardy. Her thoughts went back to those other times in her life when it was torn apart by the desire for England's crown.

What was there about this symbol which meant death and suffering for so many? Surely power was a terrible thing.

First her father's struggles to attain it, then her mother's efforts on behalf of her son, followed by Uncle Richard and his death in battle. Now her husband for the second time saw his position threatened. She sighed, but determined to make life bearable for the children confined within those grey walls.

It was her younger son Henry who came to her one day as she sat watching him and his sister playing in the small garden of the Tower.

'Mother, let me go and fight with my father.'

She looked at the five-year-old boy so recently made Duke of York, her eyes bright with the tears she tried to hide. What a fine figure he made, her little son, standing there, his sturdy legs planted apart, his rosy face with its alert gaze and firm small mouth lifted confidingly to her.

'Thank you, my son,' she said and endeavoured to give due importance to his request, 'but your father has left you to guard me and your sister until he can be with us again.'

He eyed her almost defiantly.

'I am no girl to stay with women.'

Elizabeth sought for some suitable answer.

'At this time women feel the need for some male creature of their own family to give them courage,' she said soothingly.

He relaxed then.

'You need not fear when I am with you,' he said proudly.

She watched him return to the attendants who guarded him and her heart was alive with delight in his young spirit. With Arthur away in Ludlow she realised he aimed to take his brother's place and she exulted in his boyish courage.

Meanwhile Warbeck once again crossed the border and besieged Norham Castle, but the Earl of Surrey met and overcame him so that, once again, he retreated back to Scotland. There he was met by the Lady Katherine, who had waited anxiously for news.

None had reached her from England and she was tortured by hopes and fears alternately. Was he advancing towards the goal he had set himself? Were the English joining his Scottish troops to aid him in his great enterprise? Were they willing to accept him as their rightful King or was he even now lying on some battlefield staring at the sky with sightless eyes. Katherine's fertile imagination ranged freely over all possibilities and she knew wild hope and fearful despair in turn as the days passed.

Then one evening from her window she saw a company ragged and dirty winding its way towards the castle. The men walked dragging their feet as they stumbled along the rough track and in their midst rode a solitary horseman drooping in the saddle the reins lying loosely on the neck of his weary mount. With tear filled eyes Katherine watched until the demoralised company disappeared from her sight.

It was an hour later, an hour filled with anguish for his tortured wife, that

Warbeck entered the chamber, and she flew to meet him frantically.

'Husband,' she sobbed and looked into his ashen face. He looked back at her, the pale countenance, the unshaven beard, the deep lines beneath his eyes all speaking of intense weariness.

'The Earl of Surrey surprised my men as they waited for the dawn and we were forced to retreat. Katherine, I must tell you something which grieves me. We must part.'

She stared back at him, grey eyes meeting blue.

'Part?' she faltered. 'Oh, no!'

His hands clasped hers.

'I have just seen the King,' and he choked as he spoke. 'James has spoken terrible words to me. Twice now the English have rejected me, once in Kent, the second time now at Norham. He sees no likelihood of them ever accepting me and says that he will now withdraw his troops and make peace with England. In vain I begged him to think again — he is adamant. Only granting me safe conduct out of this country.'

Katherine spoke in determined tones.

'I will go to the King and plead with him.'

He restrained her.

'My love, before I left him he sent a message to you. "Tell the Lady Katherine that I will hear no outcry from her. She is welcome to remain here if she so desires, but should she go with you she is no longer under my protection."'

The colour rose in her face.

'I love you deeply. Remember the words of Holy Writ when Ruth spoke to Naomi her mother-in-law 'Whither thou goest I will go. Thy people shall be my people and thy God my God.' So I feel for you.'

His eyes were wet with tears as he kissed her hands.

'Katherine my wife — my all. When I win my kingdom you will be my most treasured possession.'

He left her then to seek his couch

and as he sank into troubled slumber she sat beside him, listening to the mutterings of a distressed mind. Steadfastly she reiterated silently the promise she had made to him. Always to remain with him, her love wrapping him round like a mantle to shield and protect. Doubts and fears as to the justice of his cause did not concern her. It was enough that they should be together in success or failure and she would never question him as long as they lived. She stroked the unruly hair with a tender touch and felt the tears run down her face as love and sympathy possessed her.

Three days later their little body of faithful followers left for the coast and set sail for Ireland. The wind howled, the four small ships in which they travelled plunged through the tumbling waters and she lay in the tiny cabin of one, wrapped in a warm cloak, while above her on the deck he kept watch with his men.

'They fight for me, so must I bear

them company,' he said and she adored him for his constancy. They landed as dawn broke over a desolate beach and struggled towards the little town of Cork. But this time they were met with lowering glances from the inhabitants and shelter was hard to come by. 'This is no Prince,' their manner said, 'but an unsuccessful man cast off by the great ones of powerful countries.'

They found a resting-place in a deserted barn and managed to buy food from a nearby farmer with some of the money Katherine had brought with her. In sad shape they realised there was no help there and it was Katherine herself who made a suggestion.

'I have heard that the people of Cornwall are bitter against Henry. He levied a tax on them to help pay for the northerners' defence when you attacked that part of England. Let us try those fierce Cornishmen who consider themselves a race apart.'

With renewed hope and cheered by her words they again set sail and once more the weather buffeted them cruelly, but when sea-stained and weary they saw the coast loom up in the mists they found it was not the mainland but a rocky promontory called St Michael's Mount.

This little island was occupied by the lodgings and stables of a captain and his guards who watched over it. For two or three hours when the tide ebbed it became a part of Cornwall, joined by a narrow causeway across which men and horses could reach the mainland but, apart from the garrison, and certain buildings housing its men, there stood only the monastery of St Michael the dragon slayer which tended to the spiritual comfort of the fortress.

They were received courteously by the captain and the kindly monks, who came out to welcome the travellers. Perkin turned then to look at his wife as she stood beside him. Her hair fell in strands about her face, her gown and cloak were soaked from the fog and foam and she shivered uncontrollably.

With his arm round her he moved towards a brown-habited figure.

'Father, I am Warbeck of whom you have doubtless heard. I come to fight for my throne and this is my wife the Lady Katherine. She has suffered much and begs you to give her shelter.'

The grave eyes of the prior looked back at him.

'My son, we take no part in the dissension of men, but here is one in dire distress. Leave her with us until you return. She will be well cared for until you come to claim her.'

Perkin turned then to the weary girl.

'Katherine, my love, wait here until I come again. The mainland looks an inhospitable place but my future lies there and I must take my chance.'

She protested feebly but he took her face between his hands:

'I will come for you soon, doubt it not,' and kissed her mouth.

Two days later, refreshed and heartened by the garrison, who had provided armour and weapons, he and his men set out when the tide was low and Katherine watched with heavy heart as they disappeared into the mist. But when Warbeck set foot upon the mainland hope rose again in his breast.

The men of Cornwall welcomed him, flocking to join his standard and shortly he set course for London with six thousand men. It was at Exeter that he attacked the northern gate but he found Henry's forces waiting for him and he lost four hundred of his company. He withdrew and proceeded to Collumpton but there found the mood of the Cornishmen had changed. They heard that Henry had imposed very heavy fines on all who gave help to 'the feigned boy' as he was called and Warbeck realised that the tide was turning against him.

On the twenty-fifth of September the King of England wrote briefly to one of his nobles from his palace of Woodstock.

'Cousin, trust for certain that upon Thursday about midnight Perkin fled from his company at Taunton and took no leave or licence of them.'

What Henry omitted to say was that the nerve of the Cornishmen had broken and they had fled back to their homes, leaving their leader alone save for his original friends. He fled to Beaulieu Abbey, demanding sanctuary, and there the King's forces surrounded the place. He surrendered a few days later upon a promise that his life should be spared.

One prisoner who was also taken was the woman hiding on St Michael's Mount, and it was in a letter to his wife that Henry showed benevolence. He wrote that the imposter's wife was free of guilt and being of Scottish royal blood he intended to put her into Elizabeth's care.

So the Queen prepared to meet Lady Katherine at the Tower one autumn morning and stood waiting to receive her.

Henry had treated her in a kindly manner. She rode with an escort, not as a prisoner, and, as she dismounted, Elizabeth felt great pity on seeing the fatigued countenance of the beautiful woman. But before she could give expression to her feelings Katherine rose from a deep curtsey to survey her with a defiant expression.

'Madam I love my husband. All who are not with him I count my enemies. I must speak thus to you so that you may understand my position.'

Elizabeth could see that pride was being expressed as well as love for Warbeck and spoke gently,

'You are welcome, Lady Katherine. What lies between you and your husband will always receive understanding from me.'

The other's gaze faltered and the Queen saw the tears rise suddenly in her eyes. She covered her face with her hands, but Elizabeth saw the drops flow between her fingers and was conscious of compassion for her. Dismissing the guards she put a kindly arm round her, leading her away to prepared apartments far from where her husband was to be imprisoned. There she remained, receiving sympathy from all, while she endeavoured to gather together what remained of her shattered life.

Elizabeth now welcomed her husband home again and as the days shortened the imposter rode through the streets of London still clad in his rich garments. Little goodwill was shown him by the people of the capital and they watched him impassively, noting his woebegone looks. As he entered the gateway of the Tower those who stood at the entrance muttered and jeered under their breath, adding to his misery.

The Christmas season was now at hand and the royal family took up residence at the Palace of Sheen to celebrate the festival.

Arthur had returned from Ludlow for the occasion and his parents delighted in this grave young prince who spent long hours at his books as if anxious to be proved worthy of the high position he would one day occupy. Only Elizabeth watching him with a maternal eye felt anxiety touch her lest he overtax his strength.

On December the twenty-second the Court was gathered in the great hall of the palace. Outside the wind howled round its walls but within was light and warmth and the family sat together among the colourfully dressed members of their immediate circle. Courtiers with their ladies, jesters, and members of the household stood in small groups exchanging conversation, and their laughter broke out in little bursts of sound above the music in the musicians' gallery.

The heir to the throne sat beside his mother on a low dais, his elbow resting on the arm of her gilded chair, while his sister Margaret close by showed her father a new book produced from Caxton's press. It was the seven-year-old Henry, circulating about the ladies of the bedchamber and their escorts, who first raised the alarm.

He saw two of the King's attendants, consternation on their faces, enter in haste, while behind them wisps of smoke curled ominously. Always ready to be first with news good or bad he raced across the floor, shouting loudly at the top of his voice and, through the half-open door, his father saw the tongues of flames beginning to lick the hangings.

Fearfully, Elizabeth collected her children and, aided by her husband, they made their way down a back stairway into the blustering wind and darkness of the December night. There with their dogs about them they watched with the rest of the assembly the flames leaping into the air, fanned by the strength of the wind.

The robes of the spectators were grimed by the black smoke, their faces streaked with soot, and the children watched in fascinated horror while Elizabeth wept openly as one of their most beautiful homes, filled with treasures, was reduced to ashes.

Safely back at Westminster Elizabeth spoke to her husband.

'Henry, be thankful no lives were lost.'

He puffed out his lips wryly.

'You are right, Elizabeth, but Sheen was my greatest joy. Now it is gone but I promise I shall rebuild it. This time I will give it the name of Richmond after my title before I became King.'

Part III

Elizabeth the Well Beloved

The year of 1497 drew to its close and in the New Year tidings were received from Spain.

Ferdinand and Isabella wrote once again about the uniting of their youngest daughter with prince Arthur but now the name of the little Earl of Warwick was brought into the discussions.

The Spanish King and Queen had watched with alarm the invasion of Perkin Warbeck and his subsequent imprisonment in the Tower and their ambassador had drawn attention to another who also resided there. He pointed out that the son of the Duke of Clarence, although attainted, could be a ready figure for any who wanted to take up his cause, and the royal couple agreed with him.

They were not anxious to send their

daughter to become Queen of a country riddled by continual uprisings.

Another matter which claimed Henry's attention was that of the Scottish King. James, realising that he had damaged his reputation by championing Warbeck's cause, now put forward feelers for marriage with the Princess Margaret and while it was being considered Elizabeth knew she was again with child.

Looking upon her second daughter the happy mother touched the baby face lovingly and saw Elizabeth Woodville's lineaments reflected.

'This one,' she told her husband, 'can be many years with us before being affianced. We will call her Mary.' Later she enlarged upon her thoughts.

'I do not wish Margaret to leave us yet. Twelve is too young to send her away if this arrangement with Scotland is ratified.'

Henry nodded his agreement then broke into anxious speech.

'Once again I am troubled. This

Warbeck, although imprisoned in the Tower, still continues his plotting. My spies tell me that, being housed in the room above Edward's, he is in secret touch with the young man and a certain guard named Reymond is the link between them. It is feared they plan to escape from the Tower together.'

He paused and met his wife's eyes.

'They play a dangerous game. By linking himself with the imposter, Edward of Warwick lays himself open to punishment.'

Elizabeth spoke impulsively.

'Edward is not capable of such thoughts, Henry. He is too disturbed in his mind to understand the other's plans. He can only follow like a child unknowing of what is implied by it.'

Henry's mouth tightened ominously.

'He is twenty-four years of age, not a child. Should he let Warbeck influence him he must expect to suffer.'

Elizabeth feared she understood the tortuous workings of Henry's mind. Suffering as he had through the machinations of two imposters he sought an end to any more trickery. He cared not now for Perkin, he was a spent force and could be dealt with at any time, but Edward was different.

As she herself had been legitimised so the attainder against his father Clarence could be revoked and what had they then? A King in embryo. Remembering the boy's terrified tears at Sheriff Hutton she felt a cold shadow stealing over her as she realised that the weak-minded boy could become embroiled in a new plot.

She spoke to her husband.

'Surely, Henry, it would be better to change Warbeck's chamber and arrest this man Reymond.'

The King looked at her, his glance hostile.

'I know this man Reymond and will deal with him accordingly. Also no good will be served by parting them. Being where they are suits my plans better.'

His words confirmed her fears and she realised with a sinking heart that if

Warbeck involved the boy in his plot Henry could remove two more contenders for his throne in one action.

On a certain night, watched by unseen eyes, Warbeck crept from his room, and with two of the keepers strangely missing made his way to the room below. From there, holding Edward's hand, he encouraged the bewildered boy to creep down the stone steps, only to see the King's men move forward to arrest them.

Warbeck was imprisoned in a cell in the Tower while his frightened companion was returned to his chamber, crying piteously the names of his familiar guards. Two men called Thomas Ashwood and Long Roger, who had been corrupted by Perkin, were hanged but Robert Cleymond mysteriously disappeared and, learning this, Elizabeth knew he was a spy of her husband's.

Two days later, on a scaffolding erected for the purpose stood the would-be King, his garments torn and disordered from his guards' rough handling, reading in a hoarse voice how, as a young boy, he had left his parents' home in Tourney and travelled to Cork, where, encouraged by his likeness to a member of the Yorkist family, he had been led into evil-doing. Twice he repeated this and was thereupon fettered in the stocks before Westminster Hall where he remained for two days before being returned to his cell.

On a sunless morning the crowds gathered at Tyburn, contesting for a good view, and they raised derisive voices as the prisoner was drawn on a cart to his bitter end. He tried to speak as he looked on the faces of his tormentors but their mockery made it impossible for him to be heard and he fell silent, giving himself into the hands of his executioners. A howl of delight rent the air as the cart was drawn from under him and he struggled in the awful agony of death.

On November the twenty-first the peers of the realm sat in judgement on the Earl of Warwick. The charge was high treason for, as was said in the indictment, 'intending to make Peter Warbeck King of England' but many of the nobles who were present had stood in this same hall when the prisoner's father had been sentenced in 1478 and they watched regretfully as he was condemned to death by the Earl of Oxford.

He had been persuaded to plead guilty and his bewildered eyes wandered over the faces of those who watched, understanding little of what went on.

The days following were bitter ones for Elizabeth. Her little cousin's clouded mind and his hapless end together with her husband's feared participation had caused her great grief. She saw too that the occurrences of the past weeks had etched themselves upon Henry's countenance. Streaks of white showed in his thinning hair and his shoulders took on a bowed appearance.

He was nearing his forty-sixth year

and Elizabeth, looking upon the face of the man she had married, saw all the crises of his disturbed life engraved thereon.

Now there was one unpleasant duty which Elizabeth had to perform, and, steeling herself, she made her way one day towards Lady Katherine Gordon's apartments. As she passed a certain door she heard the sad tones of a woman speaking in great distress.

'How could the King even think my brother guilty.'

A man's voice answered soothingly,

'Meg, the King was in a terrible position. He has always been merciful to those imposters who seek his throne. Now your brother's name, so close to his in rank, has been seen by the people to be linked with Warbeck's to create confusion.'

A fresh burst of tears made Elizabeth realise that she was intruding upon another's grief and, as she passed on swiftly, she glimpsed the form of Margaret Plantagenet, her head buried in the shoulder of Sir Richard Pole.

Lady Katherine, at the insistence of the Queen, had been moved with her ladies from the Tower where her husband had been confined to chambers in Westminster Palace and on this day as Elizabeth entered she stood by a window overlooking the Thames. In the distance across the fields she could see the towers of her late husband's prison piercing the skyline while the rain fell heavily as if nature itself wept for the woman who watched.

Turning from the gloomy scene without to face the Queen she dropped into a curtsey. Her eyes were red with weeping and all former arrogance had disappeared from her bearing.

'I come to offer you all my sympathy,' the Queen spoke gently, 'only as one woman to another can I reach your heart at this time. Please realise that I suffer greatly for you.'

With a sob Katherine answered her.

'I care not what my husband has done nor the rights and wrongs of his cause. I know only that I loved him and could not be with him in his dreadful hour.'

Elizabeth realised there was nothing more she could say. She had implored the King to allow husband and wife to meet but with a stony face he had refused, and conscious of the issues involved she dare not ask again.

Already there had been vague murmurings as to the King's involvement in the matter and, seeing his culpability in eliminating the two men, she dared not give impetus to the country's curiosity. So she withdrew quietly from the chamber, leaving orders that Katherine should be treated with all the respect her royal blood demanded.

It was soon after this that she knew she was expecting another child, and for the first time wondered if she would have the necessary strength to bring the babe into the world. But when the time came she was delivered of an apparently healthy son who was named Edmund.

She was conscious however that she

did not recover her former health and the King spoke of it one day to her.

'Bessy, you and I have suffered much during these last months. Now with the relaxation of our troubles we must strive to regain our health. I am taking you to Calais to visit Philip, Archduke of Burgundy.'

Knowing her husband, Elizabeth was sure that there was another reason to warrant such an expensive event and it was soon made clear to her.

Slowly but surely through his careful almost miserly ruling England was becoming wealthier than she had been for many centuries and now the King wished to prove it to the countries across the sea.

So the King and Queen said goodbye to their children and set off for the coast. Pageantry was the order of the day and the citizens watched in amazement at the wealth of jewelled trappings on horses and carts, the chains of gold about the necks of the grooms and squires and the richness of the Queen's robes as she rode in her golden coach before her husband.

'This King has been a hard man,' they muttered to each other, 'we have suffered through his parsimony but now he will show the King of France among others his power and wealth.'

With his customary caution Henry had made an oath never to set foot in another ruler's country so the meeting took place outside Calais, where the fields around were bedecked with brightly coloured tents, those of the King and the Duke showing regally beside those of their respective nobles.

There the chivalry of England and Burgundy met, flaunting their wealth and importance, while masques, tournaments and jousts were performed during the following weeks. The glittering occasions, the new faces, all aided the Queen's spirits as well as the meeting with the Duchess Juana.

The latter was the daughter of Ferdinand and Isabella and sister to Catherine, Elizabeth's hoped for daughter-in-law. Many amicable hours were spent with the Duchess and her ladies, but Elizabeth could not help but notice Juana's almost fanatical love for her husband and how she was swayed from excessive demonstrations of joy to deepest dejection by his treatment of her.

One thing Elizabeth was thankful for was that the Dowager Duchess Margaret did not appear at the celebrations, preferring to remain within her own lands. Elizabeth had no wish to see the sister of her father and her Uncle Richard and resurrect those old memories that were better left untouched. Also she did not doubt that the Duke had stopped the meeting, due to Henry's hatred of the Dowager, who had favoured the cause of one of his enemies.

So at last the day came for farewells to be exchanged and when Henry and Elizabeth set foot again on England's shores sad tidings met them. The little Prince Edmund had died at four months. Although they had seen little of him his death cast a shadow over their homecoming and the Queen pondered sadly how another of her babies had left her almost before he had begun to live.

The small body was laid to rest in Westminster Abbey and, looking upon the transient nature of life, a great project was born in Henry's imagination.

'I have in mind,' he said to his Queen, 'the building of a great chapel dedicated to the Virgin Mary. The Abbey is the only place suitable for its erection and there you and I will lie together for future generations to see.'

So in due course the first stone was laid and slowly the beautiful edifice came into being, watched by its creator and founder with a careful eye. No expense was too great for this beloved undertaking, and when it was completed it stood as the permanent sign of a King's dream translated into the beauty of stone, and was named the Chapel of Henry the Seventh.

The following months passed slowly but grief gradually grew more endurable. Prince Arthur had reached his fourteenth birthday, Margaret was eleven, Henry nine and Mary three and, although Arthur seemed delicate, he remained well.

Above all Henry the second son delighted the eyes of the court. Possessed of boisterous good health he appeared mature for his years, overshadowing his brother physically, and was a keen musician and superb dancer. He moved round the court like a young Ganymede, radiating great charm combined with a keen appreciation of life, enchanting all around him with his lively presence.

Now marriage was in the air. When Arthur had celebrated his eleventh birthday a proxy wedding had taken place between himself and Catherine of Aragon and now the death of the Earl of Warwick had removed the obstacle the Spanish Sovereigns feared.

Across the sea in Spain Catherine

had been sent for by her mother. The summons had come unexpectedly as she sat with her ladies in a chamber of the beautiful palace of Cordoba.

It was Beatrice de Bobadilla, her mother's favourite attendant and personal friend, who brought the message and Catherine knew it must be important news. She was the only child of her mother who had not left Spain for another country and she wondered if this summons meant that she, too, was to leave her home.

It seemed such a short time ago that they had all been together Isabella, Juan, Juana, Maria and the youngest, Catherine. Five happy children, adored by their parents, they had spent their young lives moving with the Court to Seville, Toledo and the other great palaces, including Cordoba where she herself had been born.

Catherine loved her parents devotedly and to her mother the youngest child was also the dearest.

Through their marriage Ferdinand

and Isabella had united the lands which had become Spain and which was now growing into a mighty force on the Continent and Catherine knew that they took pride in having eliminated all heretics out of the new kingdom.

Also, through the efforts of that fanatical priest Torquemado, the Morrs had been driven out of Granada, and the provinces' greatest jewel, the great palace of the Alhambra, could now be enjoyed by the people of Spain who were its rightful owners.

So at the appointed hour Catherine walked through the long gallery to her mother's apartment. Isabella sat in a high-backed chair and regarded her daughter with a loving eye. A feeling of sadness enveloped her but she was well used to controlling any weakness so she smiled and looked at the slender form, the brown doe-like eyes fixed anxiously upon her and the auburn hair which had been handed down from her own Plantagenet ancestry. Holding out welcoming hands she gestured to a small stool beside her.

'Catalina, come sit. I have important news for you.'

The Princess obeyed, pressing herself against the Queen's chair. The thought passed through her mind.

'If ever I have a daughter I will be such a mother as mine is to me,' then composed herself to listen. Isabella's voice was charged with emotion.

'This day your father and myself have received a letter from Henry, the English King. A certain obstacle which prevented the ratification of your marriage with his son has now been removed and we have sent off our consent for the ceremony to take place. You will shortly travel to England to become the Princess of Wales and future Queen of England.'

Catherine held tightly to her mother's hand, the tears rising.

'Mother, I must leave you. I cannot feel happiness at that.'

The Queen spoke firmly.

'You are going as ambassadress for

Spain as well as a future Queen. By your behaviour in England you will advance our country's prestige and make the people love you.'

Catherine was dismissed then with a loving kiss and as she went back to her chamber her mind was on the great change that was to take place in her life. England! A cold and sunless country, she had heard, with a mean King who watched continuously to see his subjects did not overspend. Of his Queen little was known and of her future husband Arthur and his brother and two sisters even less.

She paused to rest her arms on the balustrade of the open gallery, staring out across the courtyard below. The sun shone down on graceful statues dotted about among the orange trees heavy with their golden fruit but the fierce heat was tempered by the sight of the sparkling fountain falling gracefully into a marble bowl in which swam gaily coloured fish.

But her thoughts were far away with

her childhood playmates. Her sister Isabella now dead in childbirth, her brother Juan carried off by a deadly fever, Juana and Maria far away and wedded.

Catherine knew that her mother suffered much sorrow over Juana. There had been insanity in the family through her maternal grandmother, Isabella of Portugal, and the Queen always feared that this terrible scourge would reappear in one of her children. Juana had married Philip, Archduke of Burgundy, and there had been strange reports of the behaviour of the Duchess, especially since the birth of her son Charles. Mother-love apparently meant nothing to her, all her affection was centred upon her husband Philip, and her clinging love was alienating him so that he spent long periods away from her. This but heightened her unnatural behaviour and she continually made terrible scenes in which she begged him hysterically to make love to her. This drove him even farther away, so that he turned to other women of the court and it was rumoured that one in particular attracted him.

Catherine remembered a terrible tale which had leaked out of how her sister had confronted the lady, acting in a demented way. She had scratched and bitten her face and pulled her about the chamber by her locks. So strong had been her frenzied grasp that she had torn handfuls of hair out by the roots, reducing the Duke's favourite to a state of sobbing tears. The result was that Philip gave orders that the door between their sleeping apartments should be locked and the members of the court heard the ominous sounds as his wife assaulted the stout wood with fists and feet. When her strength gave out she lay weeping hysterically until her attendants carried her away.

The young girl sighed and turned to move on. As she did so a hand was on her arm and a voice spoke in her ear.

'Why so pensive, Catalina?' and she turned to welcome the newcomer. It was her greatest friend, Maria de Salinas, the daughter of a high nobleman at court, and she answered her impulsively,

'Maria, oh Maria, I am to go to England to be the wife of the Prince of Wales. I know not whether I am glad or sorry.'

Maria's black eyes shone. She was a lively, brilliant girl and with her quick mind and impetuous nature was a perfect foil to the princess's more placid nature. She threw back her head and laughed delightedly.

'You will take many ladies with you, my dearest. Surely I will be chosen as one of them.'

Catherine's eyes brightened.

'Oh, yes, Maria, I will request my mother that you should accompany me. Then I shall have one at least whom I love to be with me when I am Queen of England.'

Maria's face grew serious as she spoke quietly, her arms about the princess.

'Catalina, never will I leave you. If ever we are parted I will find some means to come to you. This I promise from my heart.'

She spoke with such conviction that Catherine laughed and hugged her.

'If ever I stand in such need, thank you, but I do not fear such a future. Only I am sad that I must leave my mother and travel to that cold and distant land.'

So the Princess with her parents' blessing set sail for England.

Elizabeth had written to the young bride in heartfelt words, promising that she would receive her with love and pleasure and waited now to receive her new daughter. At first, the arrival was delayed by raging storms which had driven Catherine's ships back to the coast of Spain, but then came glad news that she had landed safely and was on her way through England.

Two days before her expected arrival in London a strange event occurred which puzzled Elizabeth. The King had departed on horseback with a small company of attendants, leaving only a message that he would be returning within a day or so, and when he reappeared on the second morning she met him in her chamber.

He spoke cheerfully.

'My mind is greatly relieved, Bessy. As you know, all our knowledge of this princess is but the adulation of ambassadors anxious to promote the marriage. I have pondered much in my mind lately, seeing her sister Juana's behaviour, as to the accuracy of our information.

'What if Catherine was mentally afflicted and we had not been told of it, had twisted limbs or pock-marked face. I would not have our son marry where such blemishes could be transmitted to his children. So I rode to Croydon where the Spaniards lay that night and demanded to see her.'

Elizabeth gasped.

'Henry, what happened.'

'Her duenna informed me that the

Princess had retired for the night and could not be seen at that late hour. Yes, they defied me, which made me more resolute to have my way. Those Spanish women who protect Catherine are an unlovely lot and I thought if their young mistress was like them it would be a sad day for our son. So I told them bluntly that they were in England now and my will ruled here.

'Eventually they brought her forth wearing a great cloak and a dark veil, but at my insistence they removed them so I could see her as she was.'

He drew a deep breath.

'Bessy, she is everything we wished for. Her hair is fair, unlike many Spaniards, her eyes brown, and nature has shaped her with loving care. She extended her hand to me, curtseying gracefully and I could see the erect form, the rounded arm and swan-like neck. She spoke calmly, smiling into my face in true daughterly fashion. Let us hope she is as fecund in childbirth as she is buxom and bonny to look on.'

Elizabeth wondered what would have happened had his worst fears been realised. He could hardly have sent the Princess back to her parents at this late stage, but, knowing her husband, she concluded that he would have argued that her parents' share of the marriage portion should be increased.

The November morning of 1501 dawned cold but clear and as the royal couple and members of the entourage took their places in the great hall of Baynard's Castle they could hear the stir and murmur of the gathering crowds outside its gates.

Catherine had entered London to be met by a welcoming party from the Court headed by Prince Henry suitably horsed. He was magnificent, resplendent in a tunic and cloak sewn with precious stones, the leathers of his destrier embellished with gold. With his upright bearing and handsome face he gave the appearance of a young man instead of the boy he was.

Catherine herself was seated on a fine

black mule, its saddle of scarlet, her veil embroidered with tiny pearls in the shape of flowers surmounted by a hat with a circular brim, her hair flowing over a velvet cloak.

The fifteen-year-old girl's eyes were bright as the stalwart figure riding towards her leaped from the saddle and came to kiss the hand she extended to him.

She spoke a name in her broken English 'Ar-thur?' and he shook his head, his eyes alight with mischief. It was the Earl of Oxford riding beside her who spoke sharply.

'The Duke of York, Princess. Your future husband awaits you at the wedding ceremony.'

The deep colour of embarrassment rose in the girl's face as she struggled to interpret his meaning and the young prince smiled at her reassuringly as he remounted to lead her procession on its way.

At St Paul's she entered the cool sanctity of its great nave to offer thanks to God for her safe arrival and when she left she found a handsome litter awaiting her.

The people, filled with curiosity, blew on their chilly fingers and craned their necks to see this bride of the heir to the throne, she who one day would be their Queen. They criticised the strange dress of her ladies and the dark haughty countenances of their escorts, but for herself there was nothing but praise. Something in the shy, charming girl won their hearts and they never withdrew their affection through all the troubled years ahead.

Catherine herself was conscious of their approval, although she realised to her dismay that she understood nothing of what they shouted save her name. Why, oh, why, she wondered, as she waved her hand, had her parents in all the care taken to observe protocol forgotten that she understood little English?

Elizabeth, standing beside her husband, watched the figure of her daughter by marriage enter and saw how gracefully she curtsied first to the King, then to herself. Moving forward she spoke swiftly.

'Welcome, my dearest Catherine, to your new country,' and kissed her warmly on both cheeks.

For a moment Catherine's hand clung to the Queen's. Elizabeth had spoken in the Latin tongue so familiar to Spanish ears and, gratefully, her new daughter raised her eyes to meet the blue ones smiling upon her. So this was the mother of her future husband and also that beguiling youth who had met her at the gates of London, thought Catherine. How could she have made such a mistake as to think that he could be her bridegroom. She recollected now her mother's words to her 'You will not see the Prince of Wales until you meet him at the wedding ceremony.'

On November the sixth the marriage took place and in brilliant sunshine the cavalcade set off.

First, the musicians in their scarlet

tunics bearing the insignia of the red and white roses on their breasts. They marched carrying their instruments followed by the nobles of the Court, riding in single file each with the banner of his house born before him by a herald.

Then came Prince Henry on a white destrier which he made toss its head and rear and buck, to the delight of the crowds admiring his superb horsemanship. More marching men, and following them Henry's Yeoman of the Guard clad in their damask jackets embroidered with vine branches and the red rose.

They preceded the King riding on a superb black charger accompanied by those nearest to him in blood and rank, his velvet surcoat ablaze with gems, his cap decorated with curling plumes.

Finally there was a chariot, its seats cushioned in cloth of gold, drawn by four white horses, and as the populace saw who rode within their cries were redoubled.

Elizabeth's dress was of purple satin, the train rippling from her shoulders in folds of velvet while Catherine looked every inch the Princess of the great house she came from in her gown of gold tissue. She wore a circlet of multi-coloured precious stones on her head from which her light auburn hair fell to her waist, betokening her virginity.

Within the Cathedral of St Paul's the young Prince of Wales waited, the trumpeters standing at vantage-points where they could see the arrival of the royal party, and a great fanfare rang out as they appeared in the massive doorway.

So the ceremony went forward and Elizabeth, watching, experienced mingled emotions of joy and sorrow. What did the future hold for the young couple, she wondered. How would they deal with all the troubles which would surely beset them as Sovereigns? Would Catherine be a loving, fertile wife? She knew so little of this Spanish Princess.

As his mother, her knowledge of Arthur's nature told her he would be a faithful, caring husband and her heart cried out within her as she genuflected to the Host.

'Blessed mother of God, give them strength to bear whatever the future may hold in store for them.'

But as she left the church her thoughts took a happier turn.

After the wedding banquet the floor was cleared and the celebrations began. For the first time the Court of England heard the castanets, those strange clicking instruments so skilfully manipulated by the bride and her ladies as the onlookers watched spellbound. Then Arthur danced, first with his bride and then with his sister Margaret.

The scene was a vivid picture of moving figures, King and Queen, Lords and Ladies, Spanish dons and duennas all wheeling and turning in a traditional dance of the Court, and the Englishmen noted with satisfaction that the foreigners had taken the trouble to become familiar with the steps.

When it was over and the chattering throng had left the floor the young Duke of York bounded into view. So overcome was he by his own skill and the excitement of the dance that he tore off the velvet tunic he wore and danced alone in his silk shirt to the excited shouts and rythmical clappings of both Spanish and English spectators.

Flushed with success and exertion he retired and the Court masqueraders took over, acting out a play by Master Skelton the laureate playwright in which the characters were a necromancer or sorcerer, the devil, a notary, and figures representing simony and avarice.

This was followed by a comedy in which a favourite custom allowed all who wished to join in the scene and offer their own wit for the entertainment of the audience. One who availed himself of this licence and caused much mirth by the witticisms of his tongue was a youth named Thomas More. He was currently living in Cardinal Morton's household and his sparkling humour found much favour among those who listened.

It was growing late as the Duchess of Norfolk and Princess Margaret took the bride's hands and led her to the bridal chamber. As they followed, the Duke of York spoke to his brother,

'You have a lovesome maiden, Arthur. I envy you.'

The fifteen-year-old smiled faintly. His face was pale, his eyes ringed with fatigue.

'Catherine is sweet, but I have no great desire in me,' he confessed.

The other clapped him heartily on his shoulder.

'Go to, Arthur, make a woman of this virgin. She is Spanish and the women of that country are known to be hot-blooded. She will not be behind you in love play.'

Their mother watching, wondered of what they spoke, and, disdaining to take part in the buffoonery attending the bridal chamber, went to her own room to think and plan for their future.

The following days were happy ones. Despite the November weather the Court enjoyed itself with elaborate banquets, watching morris dancers and tumblers while silver-tongued poets recited their compositions, competing with the doggerel of the jesters in their cap and bells.

One morning a great procession of richly decorated barges bore the King and Queen down to Richmond Palace, newly risen from the ashes of Sheen. The Thames, alive with craft of every shape and size, each displaying its owner's own particular choice of hangings, and the sun shone, though with little heat, upon the decorations.

The royal couple were accompanied by the Prince of Wales and his bride, and Elizabeth smiled as she observed how they sat hand in hand, taking great delight in each other's presence.

It was not until later that the Queen and Catherine were able to speak alone together. The weather changed when they reached their destination and as the angry rain beat against the windows the family gathered in the great hall, occupying themselves with various indoor pursuits such as the marteaux, games of cards, and the knocking over of ivory ninepins.

Taking advantage of a pause, Elizabeth drew Catherine to a seat apart, from which they could feel the warmth of the flames leaping in the great fireplace.

'Catalina, my daughter, are you happy?'

The old loving name spoken once more in the familiar Latin tongue brought a smile and a tear to the girl's face and she answered eagerly,

'Madam, I am content. My husband is kind and gentle and I feel great affection for him.' Somehow the answer did not satisfy the older woman and she went on gently,

310

'Life will be even more wonderful when you know you are to become a mother.'

The colour suffused the Princess's face and her voice trembled as she answered, 'That is a joy of which I am as yet ignorant.'

The evasive answer caused Elizabeth's heart to sink. Above all, this marriage must produce children, and knowing her son's physical health was not of the strongest, she was conscious of anxiety. She had seen at the wedding feast when he partnered his sister how his strength had barely lasted out the dance. Could it be that the girl beside her was still a virgin and that there had been no consummation of the marriage?

But delicacy forbade her probing further and she covered the young girl's hand with her own, speaking comfortingly.

'Be patient my dear. These are early days.'

Catherine's fingers stiffened under

the kindly clasp and she spoke constrainedly,

'We are young and I am ready when my husband needs me.'

Elizabeth said no more. She sensed the fierce pride of the Spaniard and would not add to its sense of injury.

As the weather improved, preparation began for the journey to Ludlow. It was there that the young couple were to take up their position as Governers of Wales and, as the Queen kissed the bride farewell, the girl smiled into her eyes as if begging forgiveness for her prevarication.

'Arthur and I feel much pleasure in each other's company. I am encouraged by the events of last night. All will come right in time,' she said.

So the two departed and the Court turned its mind to the business of another ceremony.

On this occasion the twelve-year-old Princess Margaret was married to James, King of Scotland, with the Earl of Bothwell standing proxy. But her mother had been promised by the King that at least two years should elapse before the Princess left England for her formal wedding and new role as Queen of Scotland.

With this ceremony concluded the family could relax. Messages came regularly from Ludlow and, as the last of the winter gave way to spring, the Court moved to Greenwich to allow for the cleansing of the palaces used during the winter months.

Elizabeth loved Greenwich. From there one could smell the sea, survey the fields and pathways so ideal for long days in the saddle, and walk in its gardens plentiful with the early spring flowers. It was as if the season was welcoming the Court with its burgeoning fertility and she was conscious of increasing pleasure.

One day in early March she strolled among the marble seats and sunken pools with their colourful fishes. A little wanton breeze caught the veils and headdresses of herself and her ladies as if playing a game with them, while the men's short cloaks, rising above their ears, threatened to sweep their caps from their heads.

Laughing and dishevelled, the royal party took refuge in the palace, gathering in little groups to discuss the weather, and later when the meal had been eaten they danced and listened to the music of the minstrels playing in the gallery above them.

It was a contented company that returned to their own chambers, while the satisfied Queen bade good night to her husband, thinking happily of the past days activities. He had appeared relaxed during the celebrations although she knew his mind always turned to the hope of a child by the young couple and she wondered if even now one was in being within Catherine's womb.

She smiled sleepily to herself as she lay in relaxed comfort in the great bed, her thoughts turning to her rumbustious younger son. He was destined for the Church and for a moment doubt stirred in her breast as to his suitability for such a position.

One so independent in temperament as he, his popularity so great amongst all the varied characters in his father's court, from the most notable cleric to the smallest page! How would he settle into the sober atmosphere of such an august body as that of the Church? Time alone would tell. Elizabeth gave a little sigh of contentment and sank into peaceful slumber.

It was much later that she came out of a dreamless sleep to the sound of urgent tappings on her door. She opened her eyes as her chief lady approached the bed. Her hair was unbound, her bedrobe loosely fastened and, as Elizabeth stared up at her, she spoke in agitated tones to her mistress.

'My Lady, the King has sent for you to attend him immediately. There is a messenger arrived from Ludlow.'

With stunned feelings Elizabeth allowed herself to be helped from the bed, standing while a robe was wrapped round her and slippers placed on her feet. Her heart thudded as a remorseless fear throbbed in her mind.

'Arthur, Arthur.' She half sobbed the name under her breath as with shaking limbs she hurried along the corridor so strange looking as the early morning light seeped between the tapestry-covered windows.

At the door of the King's chamber stood a number of half clad figures, their familiar faces white and shocked. They parted to allow her to enter and as she did so the King's confessor came towards her with upraised hand. She swayed and her ladies closed round her but she waved them away, entering the chamber as a harsh voice spoke,

'Shut the door. I would speak with the Queen alone.'

'Elizabeth — the messenger from Ludlow — Bessy, you know what this means? Our son — Bessy — Arthur is dead.'

Jerkily the words came out, reiterating her name as if it was a lifeline to which he clung in his extremity of shock and sorrow and the Queen, looking at the face before her, was aware only of the need to comfort as if he were a stricken child.

'Henry, husband,' she said and gathered him into her arms. He put his head down on her shoulder and the dry, strangled sobs shook his frame. Conscious only of his misery she spoke lovingly, searching for comfort,

'Henry, God has not deserted us. We still have three beautiful children. He has taken Arthur to be with him but we are not alone. Let us pray for the soul of our beloved son and remember his wife so far from home.'

He lifted his head then.

'Who but you Elizabeth would remember Catherine at such a time. Yes, let us pray together.'

Silently they knelt, hands clasped, and gradually Henry regained control of himself. Seeing this, Elizabeth led him to a seat and went to the door. Like one in a nightmare she called for his attendants, then, summoning her ladies, walked stiffly back to her own apartments.

Once there the ladies saw her stagger and burst into bitter tears. In vain they tried to quieten her. All the control she had exercised before the King broke down and it was a shaken heart-stricken woman who fell on the bed in a mental agony which was almost unbearable.

In her tormented mind the early days passed before her. The joy of seeing her son grow in years with a sweetness which, remembering, struck her to the soul. His first words, his care for books and what they could teach him, his ever-present love for his mother and father, all gone, all passed away with the flight of his spirit beyond her ken.

As she lay there the ladies around her parted to let another come to her and Henry's hand was on her shoulder, his voice in her ear. 'Bessy — wife, let me comfort you even as you helped me,' and he raised her from the bed. She clung to him as he softly reminded her how God never gave his children a sorrow too great for them to bear. They must take up their lives together again and find hope in the future with the children who still lived, as she herself had reminded him.

In the midst of her grief his words gave her immense solace and she took courage from the revelation of his inmost feelings for her. They sustained her too in the dreadful days which followed, for she began to realise that, terrible as was the death of their son, it had opened a more poignant and tender dimension in the life of her husband and herself.

Arthur had died of the plague and was to be buried at Worcester, the journey to London being too great a distance for due ceremony to be observed along the road. The Earl of Surrey was chief mourner and the coffin, covered in a black velvet pall, lay in the chapel of the castle until all arrangements were concluded. Then, with a canopy above it and the boys who sang in the choir at Ludlow chanting dolefully, the mournful procession started on its way.

The thoughts of the King and Queen followed its progress as it covered the miles, stopping at abbeys along the route, until it reached its destination, where the people waited sad and tearstained.

As the body of the heir to the throne passed they whispered fearfully of the mutability of life. Not even the great could command life and death, they acknowledged mournfully.

He was buried beneath the altar in Worcester Cathedral amidst signs of great distress. He had been well loved by members of his household, and the clergy also were seen to shed tears as the coffin was lowered into the vault.

For Henry and Elizabeth and their children these were terrible days. The news had come through that Catherine had contracted the disease and had been unable to attend her husband's funeral but, thankfully, she survived, and eventually set off for London.

Lovingly she was welcomed back and, after the distressing reunion, the Queen and she spoke repeatedly in tender memory of the dead boy. There had been no sign of a babe and Elizabeth, fearing she might cause more suffering, did not mention it.

The months passed and spoke for themselves and the King's mind turned to his second son. The Duke of York was now heir to the throne and Henry found himself unwilling to return any part of Catherine's dowry to her parents if she returned to Spain.

So the King began negotiations with Ferdinand and Isabella, suggesting that their daughter should marry the new Prince of Wales, and the Queen was comforted by thinking that Catherine might remain in England.

But first the Pope must be consulted as to the granting of a dispensation, for the young couple were within the forbidden degree of consanguinity, but this was allowed to Henry's satisfaction and the contract went forward.

Now the King and Queen took up their lives again with an even greater awareness of their concern for each other, and many times Elizabeth looked back upon the events of her life and remembered the trials and tribulations which had beset her upon the way.

It had been like a book in its gradual unfolding of events, she mused, but unlike a book the pages could not be turned back.

She spoke of it one night to Henry as he joined her in her bedchamber.

'We have been through many hazards together, my husband, insurrection, uncertainty and, worst of all, bereavement. All have passed and we have survived. Only in one way can we hope to repair the loss of our little ones.'

He understood and put his arms round her, drawing her closely to him in loving demand and shortly afterwards she knew that once again she was to become a mother.

Now she took pleasure in the thoughts of the new child and, together with the Lady Margaret Beaufort, spent many happy hours conferring about its future.

The Countess had been living for some time now at Colyweston, a tiny village in Lincolnshire, but she returned to Court to be with the Queen. Time and the defection and execution of Sir William Stanley had softened still more the once aggressive nature, and tolerance with a measure of affection had replaced the harsher feelings.

The new birth was to take place at the Palace of Richmond and, once more, the furnishings were elaborate, the sheets and curtains embroidered with gold thread shaped into small crowns, the pillows of down, the coverlet of silk and rose-red velvet.

Now all was in readiness as the months went by, and Elizabeth in her apartments within the Tower felt contented as she surveyed the well-loved faces about her.

Apart from her own ladies, there was Catherine, her daughter-in-law soon to be drawn into a second relationship when everything was finalised for her wedding with Prince Henry, also that other Katherine, the wife of the executed pretender. With her noble blood she now took her place after the royal family in precedence and had joined Elizabeth's private circle.

There was, too, her beloved Margaret Plantagenet, now the wife of Richard de la Pole, showing her happiness in her radiant face.

The time was drawing near for her retirement to Richmond in preparation for the birth, and one evening Elizabeth sat embroidering a tiny garment while round her the voices of her ladies rose and fell as they plied their needles and criticised with a kindly eye the work which grew daily.

She was conscious that her bodily discomfort was increasing and, with an effort, she turned her thoughts to the sex of the expected child. She knew the King hoped for a boy to balance the son and two daughters left to them, and she wondered what name it would bear.

Henry was already bespoken, Richard? No, not that. Too many memories were stored of her uncle and little brother! Edward? That would not find favour with her husband. How if it was another girl? Surely the name of her daughter-in-law would be suitable and give Catherine much pleasure.

She caught her breath in a little groan and was conscious that the conversation around her had ceased. She spoke faintly, feeling the needle slip from her hand.

'I beg you prepare a chamber for me. I fear I shall never reach Richmond.'

Her words caused panic among her ladies, who moved into hasty action as her wishes were carried out. Slowly and painfully, she was assisted to the bedchamber and the hastily prepared bed, while the physicians gathered and a messenger was sent to inform Henry at Westminster.

Protracted indeed was the birth and those who tended the Queen felt much compassion for the agony she bore so bravely. A stir outside the door proclaimed the arrival of the King, and the long night wore itself away, turning into dawn, until at midday the child was born.

Elizabeth looked at the faces round her bed, viewing them as through a veil as they appeared to her exhausted gaze. She was conscious of loving hands tending her and the comfort of a cup held to her lips. She drank gratefully and spoke in a whisper.

'What is the babe?'

The King's voice was hoarse with grief as he answered her,

'A Princess,' he said.

She wanted to ask him why he wept. She knew now by the pathetic whimper in the room that the child was not likely to survive but never before had she known him so bereft for a dying infant.

She groped for his hand, pressing it tenderly,

'Baptise her,' she begged. 'Call her Catherine,' and closed her eyes on the world.

Epilogue

Now Henry's nature began to change. It was noted by all that his Queen's death had soured him and, without her loving presence, the harsh streak in his nature became more apparent. He busied himself at first in the arrangements for his daughter's journey to Scotland to marry the Scottish King. The wedding had been advanced since the death of her mother and, despite her sorrow, she set out in great state. On her way to the border the cavalcade was diverted to pause in the little village of Colyweston, at Lady Margaret Beaufort's home. It was Henry who had arranged this as he wanted to see his indomitable mother again and, in the year of 1503, a great company arrived in Lincolnshire.

In the reign of Henry the Fifth a castle had been built at the north end of the village by one Sir William Portor. It came into the possession of Ralph Cromwell, Lord Treasurer to Henry the Sixth, and Cromwell altered and enlarged it, living there in stately style. His household consisted of one hundred persons and when he rode abroad he was attended by no fewer than one hundred and twenty horsemen.

Lady Margaret, anxious because of advancing years to retire from Court, took over the castle, improving its amenities in keeping with her royal state, and now she welcomed her son and grand-daughter. It was Sir David Phillips, long in her service, who stood behind the Countess and her ladies as she waited in the entrance to the great hall, a stately figure in her Abbess's robes, leaning on a stick with an ivory handle.

She greeted her son lovingly, her still sharp eyes filmed with tears as she noted the white hair and lined face of her offspring, then turned to survey her grand-daughter. Margaret met the steady gaze uneasily. They had not met since the Countess had left the Court for ever after the death of Elizabeth of York and, at that time the young girl was lost in a haze of misery at her mother's death. Also there had not been much sympathy between the two, so she felt little affection now for the tiny old woman with the piercing eyes and returned the gaze with a defiant expression.

As she curtsied she felt her grand-mother's hand under her chin inspecting her closely and longed to pull herself away. She remembered, however, that the future Queen of Scotland must not behave like a petulant child and managed to restrain herself until released.

Henry surveyed his mother with admiration. Few raised that particular emotion in his breast but always she was the woman he most respected. Even his wife had disappointed him dying at thirty-five years of age and he would not admit even to himself how much he missed her. But still the Countess survived, that woman who had born him at the tender age of fourteen, and when the time came to leave his farewell was tinged with emotion.

As he rode back to London, having bidden farewell to his daughter as she rode on into Scotland, his mind began to turn to the future. There was the matter of his daughter-in-law Catherine and her future at the English Court but that could wait until he considered his own position. He saw it as an unenviable one, that of a King without a consort and sought for an alliance with a woman whose marriage portion would be large and revitalise his coffers. The Queen of Naples was a widow, but her son the new King refused to pay a marriage portion if she remarried. The Archduke Philip whom Henry had visited with Elizabeth had a sister Margaret and he now began to court her. A portion of three hundred thousand crowns was promised, but before the arrangement could be finalised, the Archduke died.

Henry's careful mind took stock of the position. Philip's widow Juana, on the death of her mother Isabella, had received the sceptre of Castille from her father Ferdinand, and the English King saw a better bargain in marriage with the new ruler of Castille. So, despite the reports of the growing instability of Juana, he offered for her hand, but even he balked at the report his ambassador brought him about the lady.

'Sire, the Queen of Castille is insane. When her husband the Archduke died she refused to let him be buried and even sleeps in the same room as his coffin. No one dare suggest another marriage and I think you are well free of such a one.'

So Henry relinquished the idea of marriage and turned his attention to his son the young Prince of Wales.

He called the young man to him and shrewdly studied him. Henry, now seventeen years of age, gave every promise of his early years being fulfilled and was now a broad, handsome youth with red gold hair and bluff, open nature. He was now proficient in many sports, a great jouster and huntsman as well as a writer of poems and tuneful melodies played on the lute. He had shown much grief at his mother's death and even now his manner was subdued as he faced his father.

Henry spoke tersely.

'The Princess Catherine, as you know, resides still at Court. I have in my possession a letter from her father Ferdinand promising to pay the portion arranged for when you marry her. What you do not know is that he still withholds the money.'

His son's brow darkened and he spoke bitterly.

'The Spanish Sovereign should be grateful that his daughter is to receive a husband and one who in time will be a King. I do not like his actions. Send the Princess home. I have no wish to be made a suppliant for her hand.

336

His father hesitated.

'You speak foolishly. Ferdinand would expect the return of the dowry paid when she married your brother. This I will not do. Until he sends his share she shall remain here and we will see what will happen.'

So Catherine of Aragon remained in England, receiving nothing from her father and the bare necessities of living from her father-in-law despite her letters to the one and pleading notes to the other. One day she requested an interview with Henry and when it was granted stood before the hunched figure in a great chair drawn up before a meagre fire. She clasped her hands nervously, striving to speak calmly,

'My father, I beg your kindness. My ladies and I have little to eat and our gowns grow every day more shabby. Our fire is small and the soles of our shoes wear even more thin.'

Her voice faltered into silence as the figure in the chair turned its baleful look upon her.

'Speak not to me of your troubles, but to your father. It is he who should pay his debts. You live at this Court only by my goodwill.'

She pleaded.

'I have written to my father many times. He does not answer my letters. I wonder if he even receives them.'

Henry gave a harsh laugh.

'He receives them I do not doubt. But Ferdinand feels no concern for his daughter. Until he sends the marriage portion I shall do nothing to help you.'

He waved her away and she withdrew to her own apartments, bursting into tears as she spoke alone to Maria de Salinas.

'He has grown into a monster, Maria. What am I to do? The Prince of Wales avoids me and I am alone here.'

Maria bit her lip, keeping back the words which she longed to speak. She must cheer her beloved Catalina not indulge the anger she felt.

'The Prince dare not show favour to you. I believe he still holds you in affection and would be happy to marry you.'

Catherine wailed her misery.

'My mother is dead and Juana acts like the madwoman she now is. What have I to look forward to when my own father deserts me?'

The situation was pitiful but her ladies strove to show cheerful faces, patching their gowns and taking them in to hide their thin figures. One day, unexpectedly, Ferdinand moved. Catherine heard the news through Prince Henry, who sought her out and spoke cheerfully.

'Catherine, today my father received two instalments of our marriage portion from your father. He is much pleased and hopes of our marriage are revived.'

Catherine clasped her hands together and he took them in his warm clasp.

'One day we may be man and wife,' he said and his eyes shone. She felt the colour flood her face and his personality overwhelm her. He was so attractive and she realised that it was not only to be saved from this miserable life that she desired him. He left her then, saying nothing more before her ladies and shortly she was sent for by the King. She was filled with horror as she saw her father-in-law. He was now a shrunken old man continually wracked by a shattering cough, one wrinkled hand ever reaching out to an attendant who stood beside him holding a silver salver on which lay several kerchiefs.

'So your father has sent money, saying that he will settle the remainder half yearly. Only when the third and fourth parts arrive will the marriage take place,' and he laughed harshly, turning to spit into the bowl beside him.

She withdrew, her mind afire. How long would the King live? Would he survive another year?

Her fears were well founded. At Richmond Palace, on April the second, 1509, Henry the Seventh died and he was laid beside his Queen in the chapel at Westminster Abbey. Returning to the palace on a grey day with little sun and a piercing wind, Catherine voiced her fears to Maria.

'What will become of me? The two portions are still not paid and I fear my father will never settle now.'

She waited in great distress while her ladies tried to gain knowledge of what was taking place outside her chambers. They knew that the new King Henry the Eighth had taken the throne on the twenty-second and had been acknowledged by the people with great delight. He brought to the throne an aura of well-being and hope which pleased them after the gloom of his father's last years. The kingdom was at peace, with no war pending. James the Fourth was the new King's brother-in-law, Louis the Twelfth was King of France. On the horizon was rising the star of a certain Thomas Wolsey, who had been a good servant to the old King and was now Chaplain of the Deanery of Lincoln.

One of the first acts of the new King

was the arrest of Sir Richard Empson and Edmund Dudley, who had wielded 'Morton's fork' so successfully and, although they pleaded that they had but carried out orders which benefited the late King, they were thrown into prison to be tried later in the year.

All this Catherine learned through the good offices of her ladies, but no word was brought to her officially. She heard of the banquets celebrating the accession of the new King and one day she dismissed her ladies and began to compose a letter to her father, asking for his help. She was about to send for her secretary when Maria entered the room, her manner agitated.

'The King is coming. I have just had word that he is now approaching.'

Catherine came to her feet speaking breathlessly.

'Who accompanies him?'

Before Maria could answer, the door was thrown open and Henry stood there, behind him crowding a group of his nobles. His face was flushed, his manner speaking of the pleasure he knew he was giving to the young woman who curtsied before him.

'Catherine, I have come with happy news. I have determined to complete the contract of marriage between us arranged for by my father the late King and shortly you will become my wife. Then we can be crowned together as King and Queen.'

He was like a boy in his excitement. His eyes shone, there was no question in his mind of her refusal. Carrying all before him he turned to the men behind him.

'Here is your future Queen and my beloved wife. Pay her your homage.'

As if in a dream Catherine listened. Could this be true? Queen of England to this regal Prince. She felt his kiss on her hand, saw the light of affection in his eyes and heard the murmurs of delight come from the lips of all.

When he had gone and all was quiet she turned to her ladies happily and spoke to her friend.

'I must give thanks, Maria,' and walked into the private chapel adjoining her bedchamber.

There she fell on her knees and prayed.

'Oh, blessed Virgin, make me worthy of such a husband,' she implored humbly.

On the seventh of June 1509 the young couple were united by the Archbishop of Canterbury, Catherine wearing white, her hair falling loosely about her shoulders stressing her virginity.

A fortnight later the coronation took place amid great rejoicing, and the young couple rode together through decorated streets filled with cheering crowds who acclaimed them.

Never, the citizens of London told each other, was there such a handsome couple, never a King and Queen more worthy of their approbation. The future was bright, they prophesied, and, when the offspring of the marriage were born, England would be well guarded. So the people of England celebrated a marriage which began in acclaim and was to end in heartache and misery.

We do hope that you have enjoyed reading this large print book.

Did you know that all of our titles are available for purchase?

We publish a wide range of high quality large print books including:
Romances, Mysteries, Classics
General Fiction
Non Fiction and Westerns

Special interest titles available in large print are:
The Little Oxford Dictionary
Music Book, Song Book
Hymn Book, Service Book

Also available from us courtesy of Oxford University Press:
Young Readers' Dictionary
(large print edition)
Young Readers' Thesaurus
(large print edition)

For further information or a free brochure, please contact us at:
Ulverscroft Large Print Books Ltd.,
The Green, Bradgate Road, Anstey,
Leicester, LE7 7FU, England.
Tel: (00 44) **0116 236 4325**
Fax: (00 44) **0116 234 0205**